T0034953

Praise for Selamlik

"Anyone who has read this novel will probably never again babble about 'immigrants,' or 'refugees' if they're politically correct, in such a sweeping manner, but rather discover people in all their complexity. Literature can hardly achieve anything greater."
MARKO MARTIN, *DLF Culture*

"Khaled Alesmael reminds me of Jean Genet, brutal and hopelessly romantic at the same time."
JONAS GARDELL, *Expressen*

"Despite the difficult themes dealt with in the book, it is always full of humor and irony."
HENRIK BROMANDER, *Swedish Television*

"In the novel *Selamlik*, the Syrian-Swedish writer Khaled Alesmael tells of curiosity and desire, and the winter landscape of Sweden. With a mixture of pleasant laconicism and narrative poignancy, Khaled Alesmael does not shy away from describing the horrors of civil war or the more tangible details of love between men. One can smell both the 'slaughtered lemons' from the trees of bombed Damascus and the mixture of sweat and castile soap in the catacombs of the hammams. All this without becoming pornographic, either in terms of horror or sex."
TAZ Berlin

"What does it mean to be a homosexual man in dictatorial pre-war Syria? The author Khaled Alesmael, who fled to Sweden, talks about this in his autobiographically

grounded novel *Selamlik*: precise, crystalline and with amazing calm, without any lyrical or metaphorical excesses."
Deutschlandfunk Kultur

"*Selamlik*, which means 'a room only for men,' is Khaled Alesmael's debut novel. Alesmael's language is beautiful in its simplicity and manages to be powerful without great excesses."
Amnesty Press

"A future classic."
Dagens Nyheter

Selamlik

To My Mother

KHALED ALESMAEL

Selamlik

Translated from the Arabic by Leri Price

WORLD EDITIONS
New York

Published in the USA in 2024 by World Editions NY LLC, New York

World Editions
New York

Copyright © Khaled Alesmael, 2018
Original title *Selamlik*
First published in translation into English in 2024
by World Editions

English translation copyright © Leri Price, 2024
Cover image © Maja Kristin Nylander
Author portrait © Ben Wilkin

Printed by Lightning Source, USA

This book is a work of fiction. Any resemblance to actual persons,
living or dead, or actual events is purely coincidental. The opinions
expressed therein are those of the characters and should not be
confused with those of the author.

Library of Congress Cataloging in Publication Data is available

ISBN 978-1-64286-148-8

First published in its Swedish translation in Sweden in 2018, by
Leopard Förlag

All rights reserved. No part of this publication may be reproduced,
stored in or introduced into a retrieval system, or transmitted, in
any form, or by any means (electronic, mechanical, photocopying,
recording or otherwise) without the prior written permission of the
publisher.

Company: worldeditions.org
Facebook: @WorldEditionsInternationalPublishing
Instagram: @WorldEdBooks
TikTok: @worldeditions_tok
Twitter: @WorldEdBooks
YouTube: World Editions

CHAPTER 1

Our Room With a View

The wooden shades of my sister's bedroom, closed and covered with delicate tulle curtains, cast a soft shadow that enveloped my damp body. Outside, Aleppo was gently stirring from its afternoon rest. A breeze slipped between the shutters and gently teased the curtains, then brushed against my wet skin, and I realised it was still hot outside. I hadn't dried myself properly after my quick cold shower but I let the velvety towel dangle from my hand, the sheen of water on my chest hair glistening in the mirror in front of me. I didn't dare look up and catch my own eye in case I asked myself, *Do I really want to meet him?*

The velvety towel slipped from my hand onto the marble floor. I picked it up and started drying myself, savouring the sensation. I had been in this room several times, but I had never really given it much attention before. My heightened senses now took in the brass chandelier in the shape of an upturned candelabra from which four long lamps swung like extinguished candles. It was a work of art, framed by the delicate ornamentation around the edge of the ceiling. A double bed occupied the centre of the room, covered by a large white damask blanket embroidered with silver thread, its edges resting gently on the ground. To the side of the bed stood a small chest of drawers littered with lipsticks, bottles of perfume for men and women, make-up, and several moisturising creams, each object doubled in the huge mirror that stood behind it all. To my right there was another mirror, this one pear-shaped and enclosed by a copper frame of entwining leaves and branches. It reflected my naked body. I usually thought I looked ridiculous in that mirror – like I was a prisoner inside that big pear. But this time was different; inside that fruit I now saw the body of a boy, the son of eighteen springs, pure and virginal, in full and perfect bloom.

My clothes were in my gym bag behind the door. I squatted next to it in search of my underwear, then glanced over my shoulder to look at the reflection of my back in the mirror. I swayed my arm in the air, as though to make sure it was my reflection and no one else's. A strain of a well-known song, the name of which I couldn't recall, slipped through the gap at the bottom of the door. I plunged my hand back into the bag and fished around for my white cotton briefs. This was the nicest pair of underwear I owned, a congratulatory gift from my cousin for being accepted into the English Literature Department at the university. I drew them on slowly, enjoying the sensation as they slipped over my legs. I picked a perfume bottle at random from the chest of drawers and sprayed it on my neck, then put on a white T-shirt and jean shorts. Even in these light summer clothes, my body was sweating. I didn't put my trainers on – I was afraid of sweating even more – and instead carried them by their laces.

I slung my gym bag over my shoulder and sauntered to the living room, where I could feel a refreshing draught from the air conditioner. The room was empty except for a rectangular walnut table, a huge brown leather sofa, and a large TV screen on the wall. Syria TV was showing a rerun of an old concert. In the corner of the screen, the date and time were displayed in numerals: 10/06/2000 16:45. I sank onto the sofa. From this position I could see my sister Maryam in the kitchen. She was filling Tupperware boxes with meals for me to take to my room in the dormitory.

Maryam was eighteen years older than me. There were four of us—her, my two older brothers, and me. She had left our family home in Deir Ezzor the year I was born and moved to Aleppo to study civil engineering. During her studies she fell in love with a classmate, the youngest son of one of the biggest pistachio traders in Aleppo and the owner of considerable land outside the city. They got married before they graduated, which is how it goes for the rich. I was five years old at the wedding and would never have had any memories of it if it weren't for the video. The things that stick out in my memory: the celebrations cost a million liras, the legendary singer Sabah Fakhri performed, and above all I recall the seven layers of wedding cake covered in gold leaf. My sister and her husband graduated from university and hung their certificates side by side in their imposing house in King Faisal Street, where they still lived. He started managing his father's company, she became a coddled housewife. Her mornings were spent in beauty salons or with the manicurist, and in the afternoons she was occupied answering invitations to dinner parties, or preparing them in her own home. She had servants but she didn't allow them in the kitchen. She managed all the cooking; it was the only distinguishing feature she could boast of.

Suddenly, as I was pulling on my right trainer, the television broadcast stopped and the whole screen turned black. After a few seconds of silence and darkness, the face of a well-known man of religion popped up in the centre of the screen; his round face and pudgy cheeks were a familiar sight from my childhood as he used to appear onscreen every Friday morning before the children's programmes, and my ears were equally accustomed to waking up to his hoarse voice making admonishments and offering advice on how to please God. I was used to seeing his greying moustache sweep the words out of his mouth, his gaze fixed on me all the while. But this time was different, not just because his moustache was entirely grey now, but because every bit of him was trembling like a desperate lamb being led to slaughter; his voice was reedy and faltering.

Maryam came into the living room carrying the lunchboxes and stopped in her tracks. I thought she whispered, "Hafez Assad is dead." She placed the lunchboxes on the table and put her hand over her mouth, as if regretting what she'd said. Her body collapsed on the sofa. Again, I heard her say, "Assad is dead!" I picked up the remote and turned up the volume:

"... Today, O Syrians, O Arabs! The Leader, staunch defender of the rights of the homeland and the ummah, has passed away. The Leader has passed away … he who was so elevated in his values and his example. The Leader has passed away …"

The speech was interrupted as his voice cracked and he broke into sobs.

"The President has passed away … he who fought for more than half a century for the glory of the Arabs, the unity of the Arabs, the freedom of the Arabs, to preserve their dignity and reclaim their rights! The Leader, he who struggled against the hurricane, has passed away!"

I was thrown into upset and bewilderment. A drop of armpit sweat slid down my side. My shoe was still dangling from my right hand, and my mind tried to catch up with what was happening. This should have been a happy occasion; thirty years of oppression had just come to an end. But disappointment and frustration were plain on my face, because Assad's death had ruined my plans for the evening. Maryam noticed my anguish and asked with some astonishment whether I was sad at the news. I didn't respond. I tried to smother my whirling thoughts, but my lips eventually betrayed me and I burst out, "Why the hell did he have to die *today*?"

I got up and paced the room with just one shoe. I didn't know what to do. Somewhere amid the onslaught of thoughts, I considered taking off my single shoe and walking barefoot, but instead I found myself putting on the other. I went to the bathroom and locked the door behind me, as if chased by the voice of the broadcaster, who was shouting, "Today is a day of grief and woe in every Syrian home, in every school, in every university, factory, farm, and shop. Grief is found in every heart, the heart of every man, woman, and child, because a piece of their heart has departed."

When I came back to the living room, my brother-in-law had joined my sister. The voice of Assad's imam had woken him from his nap. The two were on the comfortable leather sofa, holding each other in silence as they watched the announcement of the end of a political era whose beginning they had witnessed when they were six years old.

The imam on the television abruptly stopped crying and dried his tears with the sleeve of his suit. Like a child polishing off a slice of cake, he smiled and gazed out confidently at the viewers, just as he did each Friday morning: "We go now to an emergency session in the People's Assembly in Damascus."

The imam disappeared.

Silence filled parliament. All the members were buried deep in their chairs, unmoving. The camera panned the chamber. The imam from the television stood, and I began to study the People's Assembly chamber as if this momentous occasion was the first time I was seeing the walls covered with intricate damascened panels and inlaid with mosaics, or the floor covered by a deep red carpet. The camera stopped when it reached the Speaker of the People's Assembly, who once again announced the affliction that had befallen the Arabs: "President Hafez Assad, known as the Lion of the Arab Nation, has died."

He asked the members to rise for a minute of silence as if Assad had died a martyr. Once the minute was over, he sat down again, adjusted his suit collar, and noted that he had received an official petition from all the members of the parliament to amend

Article 38 of the Constitution of the Syrian Arab Republic regarding the age of the next president to be elected. When he asked them to confirm the change, everyone in the chamber slowly lifted their lowered heads and raised their hands in a show of agreement.

My disappointment was overwhelming—I wouldn't be seeing *him* tonight. I went out onto the balcony for some fresh air. Still agitated, I sat on the ground among the ceramic flowerpots and plant leaves and removed the key from my pocket. A keyring dangled from it, stamped with the words *Room 333*.

June 9, 2000: Between Rooms 334 and 333

The day before Hafez Assad's death was announced, I was on campus in Room 334—my dorm room. I was staying in a unit for medical students doing their specialty training. I was the only English literature student in the building, so I hadn't found a study partner and spent most of my time in my room by myself. From time to time I would walk along the corridors and meet the other residents. The building was a selamlik: a palace where men could be free with their conversations, ideas, and bodies. They would wander the halls any hour of the day, half-naked, displaying their hairy chests and broad shoulders, or sometimes in their briefs, indifferent to the large bulges in their crotch. One might wrap a towel around his waist, not caring if it came loose and slid down from his stomach, revealing his pubic hair. Another might put on a jalabiya and raise the hem until his thighs or even the edge of his underwear were visible. They would discuss their sexual desires, their favourite parts of a woman's body. It was a new building. We were the first ones to live there.

It was a scorching afternoon and my body couldn't bear being covered. I was bored of trying to finish *Where Angels Fear to Tread* by E. M. Forster. The only thing that book was good for was to serve as a fan. I opened the window of my small room to let in a breeze. As I did so, I heard a lock turn in the room next door and, unexpectedly, caught a whiff of the same cool scent that I remembered smelling once before, when we bumped into each other in the corridor.

I had seen him a few times and had felt instantly he was going to be *someone* in my life. I knew he was studying dermatology and was training at the University Hospital of Aleppo. And he was staying in Room 333.

I quickly pulled on my shorts, leaving my chest bare. Taking E. M. Forster with me, I rushed into the corridor. Some bare-chested students were wrapping towels around their waist, talking and laughing at the end of the hallway.

The number 333 was stamped on the white, wooden door. I heard a hesitant knock, and realised it was my fist rapping on the wood. My brain quickly flicked through all the ways he might react to my intrusion and I found myself practicing what to say if he opened the door.

Brown forehead. Flushed cheeks. Broad shoulders. Large, dark eyes surrounded by thick eyelashes and bushy eyebrows. His hair was short, his beard concealing the lower half of his face except for his pink lips. He was wearing a white polo shirt with an open collar revealing the tips of his chest hair. His eyes widened as he took me in. My eyes, as they moved across his body, spotted the towel and piece of laurel soap in his hand.

"I don't feel well," I said, and collapsed.

He bent over to help me. I clung to him, rested my head on his shoulder and inhaled the scent of his sweat. I brought my face so close to him that the tip of my nose gently nudged his ear. He slid his hands behind my back and raised me up until we were clinging together, and our eyes met. I tumbled into their blackness. Ever since I first saw him in the corridor, I had traced his face in my mind and thought about kissing it. I now felt his broad palm, warm against my cheek.

"Come in. Do you have a fever?"

He helped me into his room and instructed me to sit on the bed. My heart was racing. I clutched my book as if my life depended on it. Leaving his towel and soap on the table, he walked outside without closing the door. I was alone in his room, overwhelmed with a desire to kiss him.

His room was small like mine but contained two single beds. One of them was furnished with a pillow and a blanket and the other only a mattress. In the corner there was a small, half-empty suitcase. Next to it was a mound of carefully folded underwear. It was Friday, the day when most students went back to their hometowns for the weekend. I realised he was packing to go away, and felt instant remorse at what I had done.

He returned carrying a glass of water. I apologised when he gave it to me. My hand trembled when it brushed against his, and he gently pushed me back onto the bed, commanding me to drink.

After I had taken a small sip, he said, "You're not feeling well. When did it start?"

My pulse quickened. Seeing me look frightened, he gave me a reassuring smile and said I was too young for it to be anything serious. He opened his wardrobe, brought out his medical bag, and took out a stethoscope.

"Put your book down. How old are you?"

He came close and placed the cold metal against my warm chest. I looked into his eyes as he tied a blood pressure monitor around my upper arm and prayed to God it would find something that would cover for my lies. He smiled and left the monitor on the table.

"It's fine, don't worry."

He sat down next to me. His left knee was close to mine and his leg began to jiggle; I felt a jolt of electricity every time his leg touched me. He leaned his body towards me and for a moment I thought he was going to kiss me, but instead he picked up my book and placed it in his lap.

"*Where Angels Fear to Tread.* Rather dramatic title, isn't it?"

He opened the book at random and read out loud, "Don't be mysterious; there isn't the time."

He turned it over in his hands. "Are you reading it for fun or is it part of your studies?"

At that, I began to breathe more easily. I confessed I was in my first year studying English literature at the University of Aleppo, and I had to pass this year to be able to complete my studies at the University of

Damascus the following year. This novel was assigned for Prose.

"Sounds fun," he said. "You're lucky, I study diseases."

"Yeah, I actually found the book really inspiring. I've learned so much from it. And from the characters. It's really inspiring," I gabbled.

He asked how I managed to get a room in the dormitory designated for medical students during their specialisations. I told him my uncle had been the mayor of Aleppo at the time, so it had been easy. He shifted away from me then, resting his back against the wall, and said, "I'm Ali Furdan, from Tartous."

His surname informed me he came from one of the big families on the coast. Later, he said his father had some high rank or other in the army. I always used to think families like that raised their kids to be spoiled brats who got everything they wanted, travelling and studying abroad, all paid for by the state. There had been a few of them in my class at school, and they considered the school, the classroom, the teacher, and even the students, their own personal property. Haughty and overbearing, they were usually deemed to be outstanding students for no particular reason and were spared any collective punishments the rest of the class had to suffer.

He interrupted my thoughts and offered me a hot maté. I nodded in an effort to please him, but regretted it immediately. I felt choked by the smell of maté, like dust, and I couldn't hide my distaste at its bitterness when I took a sip.

I said quickly, "I feel much better, I think. You're going away, right? I don't want to make you late."

He cut me off: "Relax. I want you to be my roommate."

He leaned in closer and said, "If not, the administration will put me with some random stranger."

He pointed at the empty bed.

Before I could answer, he took a bunch of keys from his pocket and removed one. He handed it to me and said, "Go and speak to the building manager, then bring your things here. I want to see you in this room when I come back from Tartous tomorrow night."

He placed the keys into my sweaty palm.

"I'm going for a shower now."

June 10, 2000: The Road to Room 333

"You have to stay with us tonight. The Ministry of Education announced a suspension of all exams for at least a week. There's no need to go back to campus today."

Maryam's words fell on me from above. She was standing next to me, and I was still sitting on the balcony floor among the plants. She said, "I'm sure the Mukhabarat will be everywhere, especially where there's young people. They'll be sniffing out anything suspicious, trying to see people's reactions to the news."

Unconsciously, I took the keys from my pocket as I replied, "I have to go. I want to be there for my roommate who's arriving this evening."

She looked at me, unconvinced, and muttered, "I don't get why you're being like this."

I left quickly after that.

On the bus everyone was quietly sunk in their own thoughts. I hugged my gym bag and closed my eyes, trying to ignore my surroundings. The radio was broadcasting a recitation of the Qur'an in tones of deep distress, in mourning for the country's loss. The flow of verses was interrupted every time the bus driver opened the door to pick up new passengers or let someone off.

"University!" shouted the driver. I opened my eyes and thought I was the last passenger until I turned around and saw a man sitting in the backseat. I got off the bus and the man followed me.

I sped up as I entered the dormitory gates. The man carried on his way outside. The campus garden was tranquil. There wasn't a single person in this place usually filled with laughter and loud conversation. I hurried even faster. My only wish was to reach Room 333, open the door, and inhale the smell of him. With every step, I sank further into my private fantasies, oblivious to the public mourning spreading across the country.

My only wish was to be Room 333.

In Room 333, Part 1

The heat of the room enveloped me as I removed my T-shirt and tossed it on top of my bag on the bed that was to be mine. He seemed to have left the windows closed and the blinds raised, so the room had been exposed to the boiling midday sun. I left the door open for some air. His bed smelled of his perfume. I turned on the light and stood in the centre of the room, scrutinising every detail of it. His bed was unmade, his pillow folded and thrown on top of the blanket. There were used, dried-up maté leaves in the bottom of a cup abandoned on the table beside a metal teapot and a jar with more maté leaves inside, a cassette player, and a red plastic alarm clock. Medicine boxes were scattered along shelves in among books and cassettes. A sheaf of papers covered the seat of the chair. When I opened the window a cool breeze blew through the room, sending the papers on the chair flying as the wind left through the door to the corridor. I hastily locked the door and collected the papers from the ground.

I cleaned the table and the floor, tidied up the medicine boxes on the shelves, and designated one shelf for tapes and another for books. I left his bed as it was. I took my clothes from my bag. There wasn't much: a pair of shorts, three cotton T-shirts, and some briefs. I realised he had left me an empty corner of the wardrobe, so my clothes went there. To his books, I added two I had brought with me, *Where Angels Fear to Tread* and an assigned text of theatre criticism. I tried to familiarise myself with Ali's books but didn't have the stomach for photos of skin diseases and inflammations, so I looked through his music collection instead.

Most of the tapes were by a singer called Mustafa Youzbashi; I'd never heard of him. I chose a cassette at random and scanned the list of songs: "I Missed Your Eyes," "How Can Your Heart Have Deserted Me?" I would later learn he was one of Ali's favourite singers. I was about to press play when I remembered the whole country was in mourning and music wasn't permitted. So instead, I took the tape and threw myself onto his bed, imagining the kind of music it played and picturing Ali listening to it.

At about two in the morning I was sitting on his chair with the window open as wide as it would go. The night was filled with an unfamiliar silence, and my body refused to relax. Frightening thoughts came to me: what would the country's first morning be like without the president? His face would no longer be everywhere, hanging on the front wall of classrooms in every school and college and institute throughout the country. What would happen now? The country had been under his gaze for so long, I had almost come to believe he was God-like, immortal. I checked the door was locked, took off my underwear and slipped into Ali's bed. I let myself inhale every trace of himself he'd left in the bed. Fatigue finally overwhelmed me, and I fell into a deep sleep.

I was woken by the sound of suitcase wheels and footsteps in the corridor. Sunlight filled the room; I'd forgotten to draw the curtains. I checked the alarm clock and saw it was already midday. My back, chest, and arms were drenched in sweat, and the sheets were soaked. When I put on my shorts and opened the door, I saw a group of students hurrying along the corridor, carrying or dragging suitcases behind them. I passed them on my way to the toilets, which were empty. Outside I could hear students chatting and the sound of engines running. I glanced through the window and saw a long line of buses with students clustered around them.

"Where are you from?"

I turned around to see who was speaking. A young

man in his late twenties had appeared from nowhere. He was short, and his tousled hair betrayed that he too had only just woken up. He wore glasses with thick lenses. Startled, I answered honestly that I was from Deir Ezzor.

He introduced himself as Doctor Omar. He came towards me, stopping at the window to look out, and said, "The Alawite students will go back to their villages in the mountains." Then he turned to me and smiled. "They are grieving because they thought their hero and leader would rule forever ... idiots. They're scared of what might happen now. Their man sowed a lot of resentment towards them, so they think it's best for them to leave. Particularly a place full of young people rebelling against the policies of a dead ruler. Don't you think?"

His accent indicated he was from near Idlib. I knew not to reply freely—his speech was suspiciously provocative, and I wondered if he was one of the Mukhabarat, trying to draw me out.

I left without a word and took refuge in my room. The sight of the buses outside, and that brief interaction, had finally made me notice the tension, even the danger, starting to pervade the campus.

My bag was still in the middle of the room, wide open, staring into my face like it was pleading with me to leave. I felt an urgent need to flee. My overwhelming desire to seduce Ali was fraught with danger—he came from an Alawite family, one with military authority no less. If I made a single false move in front of him, especially regarding current events, it could put not only me but my entire family in danger. I hoped he wasn't coming. Then I hoped he would surprise me and open the door right at that moment, as my thoughts whirled. I picked up my novel for distraction, but it didn't work.

I left the room to call my sister, taking E. M. Forster with me, and ran downstairs to the public telephone that stood in front of the building. I took my place at the end of a long queue of people, my book stuck to my left hand. The sun beat down mercilessly on the queue and I used the book to protect my head from burning. Everyone looked sullen. Inside the phone cabin I could see a huge man; all I could make out of him was his shaved head and his back. He was shouting but I couldn't understand what he was saying. His accent was strange. His voice rose as he hurled abuse down the receiver. Eventually he ended the conversation by beating the handset against the telephone as if hoping to smash it. The man emerged from the booth glowering, his eyes flashing, and now I saw that a thick black beard covered the lower half of his face. He passed the rest of us in the queue, screaming at us like an army officer: "Hafez Assad isn't dead, you sons of bitches. The only dead people around here are the ones who think the leader has gone anywhere."

He spat into the air—spat on God, as we say—and left.

"I'm so glad to see you." A voice came from behind me, bringing with it a cool and refreshing smell. I turned around to face the sun and squinted, only to see Ali's smile through my eyelashes. The beads of sweat on his forehead were on the verge of sliding down and in the two days since I'd seen him his beard had grown. "Let's go back to the room, it's too hot out here," he said quietly. He was wearing a grey cotton shirt and black shorts. I didn't risk clinging to him the way I wanted to, but as I went to shake his hand in greeting I found myself reaching for a hug.

Room 333 felt small with him there, and a certain friction between our bodies seemed to raise the temperature every time we moved. He sat on the chair, removed his shoes, lifted his feet onto his bed, and undid the top buttons of his shirt. He glanced down to his dishevelled bed and then to mine, which was bare.

"I'm glad you slept in the room last night," he said.

I was excited to be alone with him but mortified he knew I'd slept in his bed. He took off his shirt to reveal a toned torso and a light scattering of chest hair, and skin bronzed from hours spent basking in the sun. "It was kind of you to tidy up," he said, hanging up his shirt in the wardrobe. I couldn't take my eyes off his chest, though part of me wanted to say I was leaving and going back to my sister's house.

I turned away, clutching E. M. Forster so tightly that my hands were shaking. I was terrified of giving in to my desire. But before I could do anything, Ali drew me towards him, taking my hand and kissing it softly. I moved away instinctively, but he held me close from behind. I felt his hands slide over my arms and take hold of my wrists, his warm lips on the nape of my neck. His chest hair brushed against my back as he held me firmly against his body. I could feel his warm breath on my ears and neck. I closed my eyes and tumbled freefall into the expanse of his body.

He spun me around to face him so his lips gently grazed mine. My body, shaking with fear and want, was pressed against his, my heart pounding harder and harder. He opened his body to me, brought me in, and placed into my hand what I was longing to touch. He invited me onto his bed and, in a whisper, asked if he could enter me.

Later we lay naked on his bed, still covered in semen and sweat. His shoulder was resting on the upper half of my body, and he was fast asleep, breathing regularly. As for me, I was pinned beneath him, worrying about the consequences of what we'd done. E. M. Forster was on the floor, partially hidden by my underwear. I wondered briefly if God would bless me with a good mark in my exam. Suddenly Ali changed his sleeping position, took my hand, and placed it on his chest.

"Do you think they'll arrest us?" I asked him.

Ali started awake, got up, and walked around the table. He peered through the curtains; the sun had just set. He picked up the kettle from the table and shook it. Empty.

"I'm going to fill up the water to make some maté," he said, pulling on his shorts. "I have to open the door now—are you going to put something on?"

I got up and as I pulled on my shorts repeated, "I'm serious. Do you think they might arrest us?"

Ali put the kettle back on the table.

"If you mean the morality police, they'd never storm a room in a male dormitory just because there are two guys in there. It would only happen if a girl came into the building. Or if a guy went into the girls' building."

He laughed and said, "You know what? I've heard about a couple of guys who put on burkas to get into the girls' building."

"What about God?" I asked him.

"What kind of creator punishes his creations for finding someone to share some comfort with? Don't ruin what's only just begun. I'll make us some maté."

He took the kettle and headed to the communal kitchen.

When the darkness closed in we didn't turn on the lights and instead made do with the glow from the yellow streetlights. We made up my bed and while we were putting on the clean sheets, Ali caught me sneaking a glance at him—I was watching the muscles on his forearms as he stretched out the sheets and put the pillow inside its case. He smiled at me. I felt he was everything I wanted. The narrow room suddenly widened in welcome and overflowed with homelike comfort, even though it was barely furnished.

Ali began looking for a tape. I begged him not to play any music out of respect for the day of mourning.

"Please don't say that just because I'm from the same sect as Assad," he said abruptly. "I'm going to play my favourite song now."

He turned down the volume until it was so low we could hardly hear it, which made us both laugh. He threw himself onto the bed and I followed him. I drew closer to him. He shuffled until my head was resting on his shoulder, and dropped a kiss on my forehead.

In Room 333, Part 2

There was barely a breath of air that evening. The heat lay thickly over the city. He went to bathe and I stood in front of the window shirtless, watching

Amir Al-Shu'ura Street. It was empty apart from one young man reading a book beneath the streetlight. Students would often do so on warm nights, studying in the street to avoid the unbearable heat inside the rooms. In the window's reflection I looked at the lights cast onto the ceiling, heard the lock turn, and saw Ali's silhouette enter. Without a word he tossed aside the towel around his waist and came to me. I felt his wet body as he held me from behind, and I closed the window and let him touch me. The bed squeaked and shuddered from the weight of our bodies as we made love. Suddenly Ali stopped. He stood up and pulled out the mattress from beneath me. I burst out laughing as I almost fell to the ground. He tossed the mattress onto the floor and I flung myself on top of it. From where I lay, I could see *Where Angels Fear to Tread* beneath the bed. He threw his body down next to mine and spotted the book too. He asked if I would prefer to make love or to read, and in reply I stretched out on top of him and pressed my lips to his.

We were woken by the sound of clattering coming from the corridor. Ali leapt up from the ground and glanced at the alarm clock. It was three in the morning. The noise seemed to come closer and then stopped next to us. We could see a shadow through the gap at the bottom of the door. My heart quickened at the thought that someone might be about to raid the room. Ali's eyes gleamed in the darkness; the rest of his features had disappeared entirely. There was a sound of two hands moving against the door, as if someone was writing or drawing on it. I was frozen in place, lying naked with Ali's semen all over my chest.

I couldn't breathe. A sudden quiet fell. The silhouette disappeared. I let myself breathe a sigh of relief.

As quietly as possible I got up, drew the mattress onto the bedframe, and put on some underwear. After a few moments, so did Ali. His face came closer to mine, and I saw the fear in it. He kissed me on the lips and I felt the tip of his nose, cold in spite of the heat. We each lay down on our own beds and tried to sleep.

Some time later the neighbourhood mosque began the dawn call to prayer and the muezzin's voice filled the room as he called out, "Prayer is better than sleep." I stared at the ceiling where reflections from the streetlight continued to glow. When I first heard the muezzin's voice I felt as though he were speaking to me, calling me to be cleansed. All at once I felt guilt and relief, accentuated by the prospect of repentance and prayer. But the muezzin's voice quickly grew hollow and flat as he intoned, "Pray for mercy on the soul of our leader, our great Hafez Assad ... pray for him to be granted mercy."

The muezzin fell silent but I heard a gentle snore from Ali. I pulled the sheets over my head and tried to go back to sleep.

It must have been around seven in the morning when someone knocked impatiently on the door. Ali was more or less awake, and murmured from his bed, "Don't worry, it's one of the residence officials, counting the students who stayed on campus."

He got up and came to sit on my bed. Just as he was about to kiss me, there was another rap on the door and a man's voice from the corridor yelled, "Wake up, wake up—we're going to hold an azza for the president and you all have to join in!"

We could hear the person moving down the corridor, knocking on other doors and inviting them to the condolence rites. Ali wrapped a towel around his waist and opened the door. When it opened we found ourselves confronted by a poster of Bashar Assad, progeny of Hafez, and realised what those hands had been doing to our door in the night. Ali stood in front of the poster and remarked dryly, "Now we can have a threesome."

Ali went to the bathroom while I scrutinised the portrait of Bashar Assad. It was more or less the size of the door and framed by the Syrian flag. He wore a military uniform, and his eyes were fixed on me, the same way his father's always had been. It was the same stare that fell on me from every wall, and every schoolbook I had ever carried, and every TV screen, bus, train, restaurant, shop—even in public toilets.

I spent the whole summer of 2000 with Ali in Room 333. We watched Assad's funeral together and together we watched his son assume power. We were happy, we laughed, we played, we listened to Mustafa Youzbashi. He told me his perfume was called Davidoff Cool Water. We drank maté, we read E. M. Forster and we made love. We cried when it was time for me to move to Damascus to complete my studies and he told me I was his first love. Ali was the first man to enter my heart, and it took him five years to leave it. But he left his smell in my scent bottle forever.

"Oh God, someone on this bus has to tell them I don't want to stay next to a lake. Someone has to tell them me and my kids hate water. We even hate the sight of it after that horrific journey we barely survived."

The woman's voice brought me back to my surroundings: she was complaining about the temporary accommodation the Immigration Bureau had chosen for her and her children while waiting for their residency permit to be issued. A young man went to put the woman's request to the Immigration Bureau employee, and I went back to scrolling through Facebook on my phone. It was full of jokes and ironic posts about the death of Hafez Assad. Today was the fourteenth anniversary of his death; a day that took me straight back to Room 333 and thoughts of Ali's perfume, his smile and tears, still vividly present to me.

The bus swayed as it made its way through pine forests. It was full of asylum seekers. None of us knew where we would stop or how much time we would spend on the bus, but it seemed we were safe.

Sitting on the back seat, I took a photo of myself and sent it to my sister in Aleppo with a short message: *Everything's fine, they took my fingerprints in Malmö and they're going to process my asylum request. Now I'm on my way to the building for asylum seekers.*

CHAPTER 2

The Graveyard of Åseda

"Åseda—it's the name of a town," the official from the Immigration Bureau told me when I got off the bus. I had been alone on it for more than two hours after she had distributed families among various buildings throughout the forest. It seemed that because I was the only single male on the bus, I was the last to get off and therefore had no choice but to accept the only option offered to me.

The day was sunny, the sky completely blue apart from a few delicate white threads left behind by planes.

I stepped onto a dusty expanse covered in cigarette butts. Before me I saw a four-storey building, its façade covered in faded green paint and dotted with balconies and windows decorated with brown faces. Women, men, children, teenagers—each face bore the contours of a story it was longing to tell. One of them was from Syria, I could tell.

The woman from the Immigration Bureau opened the trunk of the bus, took out an ordinary cardboard box and handed it to me. It was so light, it seemed to be empty. I didn't know why, but its arid grey colour reminded me of the landscape between Damascus and Deir Ezzor. The woman leaned back inside the bus, then emerged with a flushed face and a blue

IKEA bag that seemed stuffed full of something puffy. She hung the bag on my finger; it was fairly heavy but lighter than I expected.

She took a bundle of keys from the bus along with a collection of papers, then asked me to follow her. She climbed the steps to the building, and I kept an eye on the set of keys in her hand; I supposed one of them was for the apartment the Immigration Bureau had provided for me. We passed the second floor and kept climbing. It was lunchtime, the place reeked of familiar food and seasonings—molokhiya, fried vegetables, toum bi-zeit—and I felt a little sick. All these mingled smells lay heavily on my empty stomach. I ignored my tiredness and kept climbing, hugging the box close while the bag dangled from my fingers. The walls of the staircase were decorated with graffiti of black cats catching huge rats, presumably as a reminder to practise general hygiene.

I was two paces behind the immigration official, or to put it more truthfully, I was two steps below her, when she stopped at the last floor between two doors. She knocked on the right-hand door several times but no one answered. She read a message on her phone. Still looking at her screen, she chose one of the keys with her other hand and used it to open the door. We went inside.

The room smelled like a public toilet. I felt even more sick. I would have thrown the bag on the ground without asking the immigration employee for permission, but I changed my mind when I saw shoeprints across the floor. My eyes couldn't believe what they were seeing. It was like a warehouse for things old and forgotten; a small, filthy space filled with the debris of shattered furniture. The streets we'd driven through to get here were probably cleaner than this apartment. Still looking at her phone, the immigration official kicked open the door to one of the rooms and herded me inside like a prisoner, my essentials clutched to my chest.

Two wooden beds without a mattress, one of them placed squarely in front of a large window swathed in a black curtain. She told me this was my room; I would stay there until I received a decision about my residency, and someone else would be coming to share it with me later on. She told me to put the box and bag on the floor and said I was lucky to have arrived in Sweden during the summer. She handed over the key to the apartment along with the bundle of papers she was holding. The front page, in Arabic, read: *Welcome to Sweden*. When I asked her about the key for the room, she replied, "Asylum seekers don't have the right to lock their rooms here."

She said this without batting an eyelid and then quickly left me to the yellowed walls and the stench of old nicotine. I had to accept whatever she said. I had no right to complain or to question.

Wearily I unzipped the IKEA bag and a mattress, blanket, and pillow sprang out. As for the grey box, it contained a stainless-steel saucepan, a bowl, a white plastic mug, and a knife, fork, and spoon, together with a large knife with terrifying teeth. I later realised it was for cutting bread. I felt somewhat fortunate in being able to choose my bed at least, and of course I chose the bed by the window. I made it up with the essentials they had provided me with and hid the grey box and blue bag underneath. My bed was the cleanest thing in the room. I lay down on it still in my clothes but after less than a minute I realised I should probably explore the rest of the place. I got up and raised the thick, starched curtain. Dust puffed from its folds, making me feel thirsty. I opened the window, leaned my head outside for some fresh air and found myself facing a graveyard.

The sight of it weighed heavily on me. Death was once again next door. I wondered what had made her choose it as my neighbour. Didn't she know that death was what I had been escaping from? That my path to Åseda was paved with graves? That I had walked over still-warm corpses and hidden among them from a hail of bullets? That I had slept on the shoulders of the dead and inhaled their smell?

No, the woman hadn't read my grave-riddled story before she met me. She didn't know that my closest friends were underground. That I only knew my father, who died before I was born, in the shape of a grave. That I buried my mother in a public park beneath a bullet-scarred tree. One by one, the people I love have been wrapped in white cloth and laid down to sleep beneath the earth. My former life came to an end in a grave. My head is a graveyard, and the past sleeps there forever.

I closed the window, lowered the curtains, and flung my body and all its grief onto the bed. I pressed my whole weight onto the new mattress, carving the shape of my body into it, wondering whether it would become a comfortable haven for my soul.

I spent the whole of that first day there, inhaling the smell of everyone who had been in this room before me. I pictured their fingers as I passed my own over the paint and contemplated the walls and the ceiling. There was a light brown stain in one of the corners shaped like a map of Syria.

A fortnight came and went, and no one joined me in the room, or even in the apartment, which contained another room with two more bare beds. Loneliness eventually pushed me out of the building, not with the goal of buying bread but of discovering Åseda. I preferred to go out in the early morning, slipping cautiously down the stairs as if I was the rat they hoped to frighten away with their giant painted cats. The amount of cigarette butts in front of the building had increased since the day I arrived. I kept going. I realised the graveyard was in the centre of the village, and the building exactly parallel to the graveyard was a care home for the elderly, as though the architect had hoped to shorten their road to death.

When I moved away from the graveyard I saw houses. There weren't many of them, and they were very beautiful, like in the cartoons I watched as a kid. But here, in reality, they seemed unmoving and quiet. They didn't even seem to contain any people. It was completely silent except for the rustling of leaves and twittering of birds. On the internet I read that Åseda had approximately 2,430 inhabitants. I reckoned most of them must be dead, as I hadn't come across more than ten in those first weeks. Was the village only inhabited by birds?

Every scene outside the asylum seekers' house was like a magnificent still life. I wanted to pierce that silence. I would set off among the trees until I no longer saw any houses. These were without question the Swedish forests I had read so much about. Excitedly,

I would hurry and start skipping between the trees like a child looking for a gingerbread house. No one was there apart from me and the birds. Perhaps they were migrants too. And because the light in the Åseda sky refused to go out during the summer, I could only tell it was the end of the day when I was overcome with exhaustion, and then I would return to my room. To my bed. I rested my weary, memory-laden head on the pillow and as if I had never seen anything else I watched my homeland on the ceiling.

"The honeymoon's over," I heard a voice say as I stood on the balcony. I turned and saw Abu Halab, my neighbour from the next apartment, curly smoke rising from his cigarette. I didn't respond. We were both aware of the other's presence and at the same time both recognised that the other was in his own world. Abu Halab looked to be in his mid-twenties, rosy-cheeked, white even teeth, black beard, bushy moustache. He wasn't handsome but there was something very appealing about his thick eyebrows and long eyelashes. His head was shaved like that of most men in the building—a haircut in Åseda could cost more than half an asylum seeker's monthly income. He had arrived in Åseda a few months before me and said that within a few weeks he had grown bored of seeing the same breathtaking views of the same landscapes. At first he had been keen to walk through the forests and enjoyed exploring everything around the building. He even found the graveyard remarkable in its spotlessness and the careful alignment of the graves. But eventually, after the scenes began to seem repetitive, he increasingly preferred staying in his room, in his bed to be more precise, eating and masturbating and sleeping. Abu Halab had acquired permanent residency in Sweden but hadn't yet found an apartment to rent, so he had remained in this "stable," as he called the asylum seekers' building.

I left him without saying a word and went into the kitchen to make tea. I shut myself away in my room, lifted the black curtain, and realised Abu Halab was right. The days had become repetitive, the forest views had lost their magic, and the filth and ugliness of the building no longer disgusted or shocked me. The depressing black curtains had grown acceptable; more than that, I was grateful to them for repelling the light that never went out during those endless summer nights. I no longer saw the graveyard as eerie and had begun to take pleasure in seeing the graves laid out with geometric precision, like small stone statues. I would look attentively at the colourful flower arrangements in front of each grave, and I even looked out for a man in a felt cap who made a daily pilgrimage to the graveyard accompanied by his Jack Russell. Every morning the man would stand in front of one particular grave and let his dog wander at will between the gravestones and flowers. If he was absent for a day, I would miss him, to the point that from time to time I would glance out of the window, looking among the graves for him and his dog. Here in Åseda they made gardens out of graveyards; in Syria, they made graveyards out of gardens.

One morning, shaking myself from another nightmare, I realised I had forgotten to close the curtains the night before. Around the edges of the window I noticed a lace of frost while outside the leaves of the huge oak tree were turning yellow, red, and orange, bidding farewell to the summer. Green remained only on the most stubborn trees. Fallen leaves were spread across the graveyard. During the night the temperature had dropped so low that I imagined the dead pressing towards each other, huddling whatever remained of their bodies together.

The graveyard somehow seemed more intimate in autumn colours. The bare branches revealed the spire of the small church in the middle. A soft breeze blew, forming vertical, dancing bodies out of the fallen leaves. Everything in the weather applauded: the foliage, the birds, even the wings of the crows that alighted on the graves. For the first time since arriving in Åseda, I felt a desire to celebrate. I stuck my head out the window, looking for someone to share this moment with me, but found no one. In the asylum seekers' building, no one else was awake at this time unless they needed the toilet, and it looked as though the care home residents were sleeping. A bike leaned against the wall of the church, the chain slack and dangling on the ground. Above everything the church clock stood at quarter past ten, where it seemed to be stuck permanently. As every morning, a delegation of ducks strutted industriously down the street.

I put on a red hoodie and brown scarf to keep off the cold. I wished I would run into someone I knew, like I used to in the narrow backstreets of Damascus. I stood in front of the mirror; the top of it was cracked but I could at least see the reflection of my beard and lips. I shrugged my shoulders so the scarf hung freely, and I left the building.

Outside it felt like I was treading on a fresh autumnal cloud. The staircase had been filled with the scent of Davidoff—even if it was only imaginary. In Syria I used to put that scent on every morning before I left the house. Standing outside the asylum seekers' building, I reached out a hand and brushed the breeze with my fingertips, and it tickled my eyelids in return. When I closed my eyes, I saw the Syrian sun that used to rise over an ancient rooftop in Damascus. I smelled the fragrance of bread, as if I was waiting in a short queue at the bakery in Bab Tuma. I could smell boiling fuul and chickpeas with cumin. My ears caught the clash and clatter of plates and spoons at the breakfast table. I saw my mother's face giving me a reassuring smile. The journey to the past required no passport, no visa, no documents.

I could learn where I was at any given moment by opening Google Maps on my phone. *In the middle of nowhere*, one of my friends replied to me from Damascus when I sent him my location. Really, I was in southern Sweden, in the province of Småland, in front of the graveyard of Åseda, surrounded by a carpet woven from dead leaves. The second I stepped onto it, the breeze died down, the birds disappeared, and the place fell quiet as if the party had just finished and all the guests had left without saying goodbye. In the stillness, a ripple of water ran in a narrow rivulet around the graveyard. I heard the drone of a few flies, and a pleasant smell wafted between the tree branches. Small mushrooms sprang up between the graves, like the fingers of the dead. A lawnmower could be heard in the distance.

I wandered among the gravestones. Immaculate and smooth, most of them were made from black stone, the names of the dead carved like an artist's signature. I felt like I was in a museum of death, or of the history of death. Most of the family names ended in *-son*. The first line of graves consisted of people who had lived long lives, men and women born just before the First World War who had died at the end of the last century. Most of the dates were similar and I assumed they had died of old age, apart from a handful of women who had died in their fifties. These, I guessed, had suffered from breast cancer. I felt like a stranger among these dead people; most of them had lived and died before I was born.

I plunged further into the graveyard, heading south. I caught a familiar smell, similar to the sandalwood incense which used to burn in the old neighbourhoods of Damascus. The scent reminded me of the weeping statue of the Virgin Mary at Bab Kisan. Initially I thought that the fragrance came from the church but I realised I was mistaken—it actually came from the fine threads of smoke rising from a small dish that had been placed on the ground. Beside it were small mounds of melted wax, all lying around a grave wreathed with dewy red flowers.

I went close to the grave, which was smooth and bright like all the others. It was circled by the remains of lotus flowers, all wilted apart from one that remained bright red. Stuck onto the grave was a colour photograph of a handsome, smiling, blue-eyed teenage boy wearing a captain's hat, from which the tips of his blond hair peeked out. He was born in 1995 and died in 2014. Beneath the date of his death a Swedish phrase was carved. I didn't understand it but I guessed that it was either a quotation from the Bible or a poem. I stood quietly, studying the youth's face. This grave was an entire graveyard in itself; it differed from the others in both colour and dates. I didn't feel like a stranger in front of this grave; his was a contemporary death, like ours, just at the point at which dreams were being born. It was too soon for this blond boy to be sleeping in an oblong wooden box, to be buried beneath the earth like a box of wishes. Finding a small wooden bench directly opposite the grave, I sat down.

I raised my head and looked at the top floor of the asylum seekers' building, recognising my window at once as it was the only one open. The black curtain was moving gently in the wind. I realised it was this boy's grave that the man with the felt cap and the Jack Russell came to visit each day. He would place a flower and light some incense, and then he would sit on this small seat to chat to the boy about his day. Most likely it was his son.

I left the place with tears in my eyes.

I began to visit the boy's grave every evening to light a candle. When I went back to my room I could see its flame flickering in the darkness from my window. That faint light softened my sadness on those lonely nights.

Having despaired of finding any of my dreams still alive, now I began to rummage for a dead hope and blew some life into it. Friendship with the dead made me forget my loneliness. Every morning I woke up longing to speak to them. From the window of my room I chatted to them about life over a cup of coffee. They all lined up and listened attentively. I felt closer to them with each passing day and I started to relax and share my secrets with them. I told them my stories, laughed alongside them, and wept over their graves. The dead simply listened, which was exactly what I needed: someone to notice me.

The truth is good things don't last. A rumour spread among the asylum seekers that the old people in the nearby care home had submitted a complaint about us to the municipality. The accusation was that we didn't sleep. Like troublesome bats, we had loud, annoying voices if we spoke, and we looked intimidating and sulky if we stayed silent. Our children multiplied and became agitated and they cried all the time. Our rubbish bins spilled over into neighbouring containers, the smoke from our cigarettes polluted the village air, and our very existence threatened the safety of the elderly. They said the elderly had priority in this village—and their orders were obeyed. I was never sure if it was due to the complaint from the care home residents, but what was certain was that all the asylum seekers in the building received a letter from the Immigration Bureau informing us they were shutting the building in Åseda within the next four weeks and we would be redistributed at random to other buildings in Småland.

On the day I arrived in Åseda, the immigration official had told me I would only leave this place when I received a decision on my residency. Yet here I was, leaving that room, and my residency application was still under consideration.

A week after we received the decision of our transfer, they asked us to get ready and pack because a fleet of cars and drivers might arrive at any moment to transport us and our blue bags to our new destinations. Outside I heard the sound of the asylum seekers and car engines. I drifted to the kitchen and from there to the balcony. When I looked down I saw almost all of the asylum seekers standing in front of the building, carrying their blue IKEA bags and speaking with a handful of immigration officials. I realised this was the day we were leaving. I was alone in the building. I prepared a cup of coffee and took it with me to my room to cast a farewell glance over my dead friends who had become like family.

"I'll miss you," I whispered to my young friend.

The same official who had first brought me to my room entered. Now she was coming to pry me out of it. She didn't ask why I wanted to stand by the window until the last second, but she found it strange enough that she inspected the window and shook the black curtain a few times. Only then did I realise she thought I had hidden something there. She shut the window and asked me to pack up my essentials and follow her downstairs.

Once again I followed her , although there were no cooking smells on this day. The usual two steps separated us, but this time I was higher. And I was still carrying the same blue bag and grey cardboard box.

In front of the building she stopped by the door of a car and pointed me to the back seat. The car seemed dark despite the clock showing 2 pm on that November day. The sound from the radio was barely audible. The immigration official sat in the front. The driver stubbed out his cigarette and got in.

"Lenhovda!" she replied when I asked her where we were going. The car moved off slowly. It started raining, big drops falling onto the windscreen. I jumped when the windscreen wipers started swiping left and right but it cleared the view. The graveyard seemed very close through the glass.

"Goodbye, graveyard family. You have gone before, and we will follow," I said to myself. I kept my eyes on the graveyard, turning my head to see it though the back window despite the intensifying rain which caused it to vanish and reappear with each sweep of the windscreen wiper. Before long, it had disappeared from view, but not from my head. Just as I had left a grave in Syria, now I had left a grave here in Åseda as well. I looked to my right only to find Abu Halab sitting next to me, staring at me with large eyes. His face was very close to mine. I could feel his warm breath against my lips.

CHAPTER 3

Dogs in My Life

Plats Kronoberg
Kategori: Fritid & Hobby, Djur, Hund

I was looking for dogs for sale on the Blocket app, scrutinising each photo in turn. I enlarged the photos until the dog's nose filled my phone screen. I gradually zoomed out so their face occupied the screen, as if my phone had turned into a cage for them. I exchanged a warm, sincere smile with each one. Only dogs gave me energy. I had grown addicted to following news of dogs bought and sold on Blocket. They were just like me; all of us looking for shelter.

The waiter interrupted my enjoyment of the puppies' faces by tossing a pizza onto the cold metal table in front of me. It caused the table to shake as it was standing on one unbalanced leg. The knife fell off the table onto the tiles and the ringing clatter filled the empty restaurant. It sounded to me like the drums of war. The waiter, who was also the cook, gave me a quick glance, then left without saying a word or waiting for thanks. I hurriedly bent under the table and picked up the knife myself. It had a grey hair dangling off it. When I raised my head and leaned the bony part of my nose on the edge of the table, the hot steam rising from the pizza hit my face and the cheese smelled like melted plastic. I moved my face back and sat on the chair, observing the hot bubbling cheese, and I plugged my nostrils with the tips of my fingers. The pizza was a featureless disc without a trace of the vegetables promised on the menu. *Vegetable pizza in Syria is like a plate of fresh vegetables, colourful and delicious, mixed with gleaming black olives, all topped with fragrant baladi cheese.* The cheese stopped bubbling. A few rings of dead onion floated on top. The golden retriever smiling on my screen was by far the most beautiful thing on the table. He was being sold for just two thousand kroner and he was seven years old. What had happened to his owners? How could they make money out of a friend who had lived with them for seven years?

I had invited myself for a pizza that day to celebrate receiving my asylum seeker's allowance from the Immigration Bureau. Now I had just over a thousand kronor in my account. *That's less than the cost of saving a seven-year-old dog's life.*

I left the pizzeria.

Outside it was minus four degrees. I was standing at the bus stop, hiding my head in my coat collar like a turtle. I had forgotten my scarf on the chair in the restaurant but I would rather be cold than see that plastic cheese again. I took out my phone; there were still three long minutes until the bus to Växjö arrived so I resumed my review of the market for dogs on my phone. I never missed a single dog for sale in the province even though pets were forbidden in the asylboende. On the outskirts of Åseda there was a large, abandoned house. Every day I entertained a daydream of buying it and adopting all the dogs and puppies for sale.

The bus arrived. I got on and sat on the comfortable, velvety seat at the back of the bus, alone. The heating was warm on my head and tickled my ears. After less than a minute a woman got on. I could only see her short grey hair from behind, and even that disappeared as soon as she sank into her seat. The bus driver set off, leaving behind two women who were running and waving their hands. They had just come out of the asylboende. The bus left Åseda and disappeared between the tall trees. Suddenly we came to a halt in the middle of the forest and a huge man got on, wearing a black woolly hat that covered his ears and a black overall with neon-green stripes. He walked down the bus aisle, seemingly at a loss as to where he should sit. His clothes had several pockets and he held screwdrivers and a lamp. At last he sat down and was still. The bus was like an empty cinema, swaying through the trees towards Växjö, the region's capital.

Asmahan

On her way back from shopping one day my mother found a tiny, honey-coloured puppy by our garden gate, looking for a spot of shade to protect herself from the inferno of a Deir Ezzor summer. She took pity on the puppy, who was no bigger than her palm. She scooped her up alongside the heavy plastic bags full of vegetables and went in through the kitchen door. "Come here, kids—I found a puppy by the gate," my mother called out, and she released the heavy bags that had dug red rings into her fingers.

The puppy stayed where it was. It seemed scared and nestled against my mother's chest. My brothers and I gathered round, staring at the puppy as if it were a miracle. "Let's keep her," my mother said, a smile flooding her face. Holding the puppy's stomach with one hand, with the other she removed her hijab to reveal her long, straight chestnut hair stuck to her scalp with sweat, and tossed the soft fabric onto the marble shelf, from where it slithered onto the floor like melting wax. My mother took the puppy to the bathroom, and we followed her as if we were a litter of puppies ourselves. Having deposited the puppy in the washbasin, she turned the tap on, and began to lather laurel soap into the dusty fur. She lifted the puppy's legs, cleaning under her front legs and between her back legs, as gently as if she was washing a newborn baby, before wrapping the puppy in a white towel and handing her to me as if she was my little sister and it was my duty to receive her. "You're not the youngest anymore," my older brother whispered gloatingly in my ear, as though this was his long-deferred revenge on me for having usurped his former position as the baby of the family ten years earlier. My mother named the puppy Asmahan after the Syrian singer who rose to fame in the 1940s, my mother's favourite. She would often remark that if Asmahan hadn't died in the prime of her youth just as her career was taking off, she—and not Oum Kulthoum—would have been the doyenne of Arabic music. We all welcomed Asmahan enthusiastically into our family. My mother fed her fried potatoes, smashed and mixed with cheese, then took her to the toilet and closed the door while my siblings and I sat in the kitchen and waited for them to emerge. The afternoon sun lit up our kitchen, and the red flowers glowed on the short curtains that covered the shelves. Behind those painted curtains, my mother had carefully arrayed clear glass jars filled with household provisions: apricot jam, green walnut jam, cherry jam, jam made from baby aubergine stuffed with Aleppan pistachios and walnuts, and rose jam, along with jars of makdous, black olives, and Akkawi cheese sprinkled with nigella seeds.

My mother came into the kitchen with Asmahan tucked into her armpit; the puppy was moving her legs in the air as though she was riding a bicycle. My mother put her gently on the kitchen table. "Don't crowd her," she cautioned us and as she put coffee on to boil she sang Asmahan's song "Ahwa" in a tender voice: *I am in love ... I, I, I am in love ... If only I was the one to pour his coffee ...* We all sat around the table, gazing at honey-coloured Asmahan and her teddy bear face as though she was a slice of cake. The scent of cardamom rose from my mother's coffee pot. Asmahan paid no attention to my mother's singing, nor to the noise all around her. She showed off her delicate pink tongue as she yawned and then fell asleep. My mother placed a circular stainless-steel tray on the table that held a small bouquet of jasmine from our garden, a clear water jug filled with ice cubes, the copper coffee pot with steam rising from it, and three white coffee cups with a delicate arc of flowers around their rims. These were my mother's favourite cups; she had painted the red tulips on them herself when she was a teenager. The tray and its adornments indicated that my mother's close friends were about to arrive. Like everyone from Mardin, my mother had a busy social life—I often felt she was the only typical Mardliya in Deir Ezzor. Small groups would gather for coffee in our house almost daily; as for the grand reception where booza cassata was served, that took place once a month. My brothers quietly withdrew from the kitchen as soon as Um Saleh pushed open the gate and greeted us with "Marhaba ya jama'a!" As usual, the hem of her long purple hijab swept the ground as she entered. I was young enough to be allowed to stay in the kitchen.

"Oh no, a dog! Have you become Christians?" Um Saleh's horrified gasp woke Asmahan from her nap. My mother picked up the puppy and put her in her lap before pouring coffee for Um Saleh. "For shame, Um Elias will be here any moment! Drink your coffee." Um Saleh ignored my mother and carried on, "It's haram to raise a dog in the house … The angels will pass over a house with a dog in it." Um Saleh pushed her coffee cup away to emphasise that our house was no longer clean.

"And others will say they were seven, and their dog was the eighth," my mother said, reminding her that the Qur'an mentioned a dog. "I have four children, and Asmahan is the fifth."

Um Saleh exploded with laughter and said, "You're crazy." I always thought that Um Saleh's desire to deem everything either haram or halal sprang from a dream of being the first ever female imam of a mosque. My mother picked Asmahan up, shooed her into the living room, and shut the door behind her. Meanwhile Um Elias pushed the outer door open with her foot and came in carrying a white tote bag.

She was shaking her short brown hair, wearing a tight black dress that clung to her tall slender body. "Furat, darling, come and take this off me." Um Elias had brought Lenten maamoul with her. She told me to take one biscuit and put the rest on the side, then she joined the others at the table.

As soon as my mother handed her a cup of coffee Um Elias began to complain, "I'm thinking of converting to Islam just to be rid of this story." Um Elias said this every time she visited us. She envied Muslim women for how easy it was for them to divorce; it had been five years since she had requested a separation from her husband, and her Catholic church was still dragging its feet over a decision. She began to tell the others the latest developments of her case, and Um Saleh was so engrossed that she forgot all about Asmahan and instead sipped her coffee in silence. Um Elias was very skilful at telling stories; in fact, it was from her that I learned the art of storytelling. She was an Assyrian woman from Hasaka. She had eloped with her husband back in the sixties after her family refused his request for her hand on the basis that he was an Arab Christian. She settled in our neighbourhood in Deir Ezzor and met my mother at the grocer's, and they became as close as sisters. As for Um Saleh, she used to evade her domestic responsibilities by visiting our house. She used to call it "the house of free women," because my mother was a widow and, in Um Saleh's belief, a husband's death was the sole method women had for obtaining absolute freedom in our society. Whenever Um Saleh visited our house, she would throw her hijab back onto her shoulders, loosen her red-hennaed hair, and open the buttons of her long dress, showing her white chest and the huge golden Qur'an that hung around her neck from a thick chain. Um Saleh reached into her bra and took out a twenty-five lira note. She gave it to me and asked me to buy her a pack of Kent cigarettes and keep the change.

"No, I don't believe it! A dog! They have all sorts of diseases," Um Elias gasped as soon as my brother came into the kitchen cuddling Asmahan.

My mother took no notice of her friends' opinions and let Asmahan stay with us. As time passed Um Saleh accepted the puppy and in fact grew so attached to her that Asmahan was entrusted to her care whenever we went to our house in Damascus on holiday. As for Um Elias, she learned to live with Asmahan but would wipe her hands with alcohol before leaving our house. Our family spent its happiest days in the company of Asmahan. She was a very sensitive dog, but strong and independent too. She always knew she had been born on the street and had the soul of a cat transmigrated into the body of a dog. She used to go out in the morning and vanish, and then come back when she was hungry. Without looking at any of us, she would go and curl up in her corner that had been furnished with a strip of old carpet; my mother had prepared that nook for her as a sort of Asmahan-sized boudoir. And after she had finished her nap, Asmahan would slink to the sitting room and sweep the place with her wide eyes, seeking out an empty space among me and my siblings so she could elegantly vault into it and sit with us to watch television. She grew up with us, slept on our beds, and followed TV soaps with us from the sofa. She became an integral part of our home.

Three Swedish women sat on the bench inside Växjö station. One of them hugged a dog; she was small and honey-coloured like Asmahan. They were absorbed in their Swedish conversation, which I couldn't understand a word of. I didn't dare tell them that this same scene had occurred twenty-five years earlier in our kitchen but with different characters. I preferred silence. I spent the whole time inside the station staring at the women. I put my hands around my throat, which was stinging from the cold, and scolded myself for leaving my scarf in the pizzeria. The electronic board above the heads of the three elderly women showed that the last bus back to Åseda would leave in five minutes.

I was the first to board the bus. I sat on the backseat, my hands and lips trembling with cold. Now night had fallen, the temperature had dropped even lower. I took my warm phone out of my pocket and resumed flicking through photos of dogs for sale on Blocket but there were no new notices. I closed the app and put my phone away. From behind the window I saw queues of migrants boarding buses to various villages around Småland, laden with large white plastic bags from the Arabic shop bursting with vegetables, bagged Arabic bread, meat, chicken, and canned food. The bus set off slowly, still only half full. We vanished into the darkness of the forests as soon as the bus left the town. I leaned my head against the window, listening to my empty stomach grumble. When I turned my face to the glass, I found another Furat on the outside of the window, forehead to forehead with me. I always enjoyed meeting myself by chance like this.

Souriaty

In mid-2012 Damascus was in the clutches of a hideous ifrit come straight from hell. The checkpoints of the military police cut the city's veins and explosions tore its people's flesh. I fled the scene and rented a furnished apartment in a slum in the Kashkoul neighbourhood, to the south of the city. Most of the area's inhabitants were poor, drawn from Alawite, Christian, and Druze communities. Kashkoul's narrow alleys and not-quite-legal buildings where fungus quickly sprang up, along with its demographics, made it an ideal place if you were a journalist documenting the revolution in total secrecy ... if you were wanted for military service ... and if you wanted to keep your head down—someone exactly like me, in other words. At that time I was embroiled in a turbulent love affair with a young guy from Aleppo called Pierre; we hadn't seen each other for more than two months because of the dangers on the road between Aleppo and Damascus.

One day when fear and loneliness had turned me into a corpse flung in front of the TV, feasting on the blood of the news, mired in sweat and semen every time the electricity was cut, I decided I had to move before maggots swallowed me whole.

Before dinner, I pulled on a T-shirt and jean shorts, slipped my feet into rubber sandals, and slunk to the pet market attached to Kashkoul. This was a familiar market on Jaramana Camp Street, one of the poorest streets in Damascus. It was lined by bare shacks with zinc sheets for roofs, their openings covered by a curtain rather than a door as if their inhabitants lived on the street. Minibuses crammed with dozens of passengers stood bumper to bumper all along the street, while sirens and the cries of street hawkers mingled with the sound of barking coming from the shops. All this chaos and movement, which seemed to be constantly accelerating, filled me with a sense of dread. I had a sudden fear that an explosion was about to roast each one of us, human and dog. To avoid going deeper into the traffic, I pushed aside the curtain of the first shop I came to and went inside. I was instantly hit with the stink of dog shit. The sound of barking rose and the dogs rattled their cages in the darkness as the shopkeeper flicked on the weak LED light and welcomed me in. I saw dozens of puppies piled on top of one another in cramped cells. Their barking increased when they saw me and they competed to poke their noses through the bars, yearning for freedom. Black, brown, and white puppies all wanted to get out. The strongest of them trampled on the weakest until they disappeared beneath the ruthless crush. It was survival of the fittest. While trying to choose one in the weak light I was startled by a warm body brushing against my leg. It was a blond puppy, small and hairy, silently seeking refuge. Although she was a very sought-after mix of Labrador and golden retriever, the shopkeeper sold her to me for next to nothing. He just wanted to be rid of the burden, given the war and the threatened siege. I cuddled the puppy to my chest—my hands drowned her entirely, just as my mother's had Asmahan—and I retraced my steps back to the apartment. There had been no explosion but I felt as though I had had a narrow escape and everything behind me was scorched earth.

I found Pierre standing in the middle of my cobbled street. He was wearing a white T-shirt with a large blue winged fish on it, beige shorts, white trainers, short white socks, and a small brown leather bag across his shoulder. He was standing in front of the brown MDF door and criss-cross iron bars of the gate, surrounded by the bloody handprints placed there to ward off envy and bad luck. My darling had come from Aleppo without notice to spare me from worry. Desire had drawn him across the firing lines.

Pierre had caught my eye a year and a half earlier in the Sheraton Hotel in Aleppo. We had both come to a New Year's Eve party to welcome in 2011, he with his peers from the Faculty of Pharmacy. He was young and fresh, like an apple dangling from a branch asking to be picked. His cheeks held the joy and sweetness of spring, his hair and eyes were black with glints of silver, and his mouth was like a velvety Aleppan pistachio. I drew him out of his little clique and asked him to dance along to the qudoud music with me. My fingers entwined with his until they melted together. Madness descended on the hall when the clock struck midnight and they turned off the lights. I took advantage of the darkness to kidnap him; I snatched him by the hand and away we ran, abandoning our glasses of red wine, drunk on kisses instead. We fled together to my room in the same hotel, loosened our ties, and devoured each other. We undressed each other and trampled on our party clothes with bare feet. Pierre and I fell in love from that first embrace; we made love to the music and the qudoud poetry coming from the party. *Pour me the wine of love, it makes my heart forget its worries: a life without love is like a brook without water*. Warm blessings erupted in our bodies, and we fell asleep as if floating on a cloud. Love woke us on the following morning, the first of the year that would see the Arab Spring, and we embarked on our own personal revolution.

At the entrance to my building we pretended to be just friends, content to shake hands while I held the dog to my chest with my other. But his face was drenched with lust. I turned the heavy key in the lock of the black iron grille three times, and gave it a push. My hand landed gently on his shoulder, and I let him go in ahead of me like any other guest. My apartment was on the ground floor and was the only one that was furnished, unlike the other three above it. I opened the bare wooden door to the apartment, and we stepped down onto the granite floor. Then I locked the door behind us. The apartment consisted of a single room—bedroom, living room and kitchen all in one, crowded full of odds and ends. The wardrobe took up most of the wall next to the toilet door, and there was a fridge and a washing machine with a TV above it. The double bed rested on tall brass columns beneath a window adorned with gold curtains. In the middle of the room stood a circular glass table on which lay a pile of newspapers, abandoned coffee cups, and a plate with a shrivelled slice of pizza. The light was on, the ceiling fan was turning, and a bier was circulating on the shoulders of the protestors on the muted television. "The electricity was cut off and I forgot to turn everything off when I went out—" Pierre interrupted me with a kiss full of hunger, thirst, and exhaustion.

"See? We're a family now," I whispered in his ear as I took his bag from his shoulder and gently handed him our daughter. He hugged her, made the sign of the cross over her head with his finger and gave her a kiss. I hung his bag behind the door and smothered them both with my arms; I only let go when the dog started trying to escape, her sharp claws getting tangled in our T-shirts. "Have you thought of a name for her?" Pierre asked as he placed her carefully on the floor. He instantly agreed when I suggested "Souriaty"—it was a silly nickname I had invented for Pierre one drunken evening. "And what are you going to feed Souriaty now?" Pierre asked, pointing at the mouth of the fish on his shirt. I pulled up his T-shirt, covering his face with it and revealing his smooth chest, and began to lick the Orthodox cross tattooed there. Beneath the feet of the newsreader, Souriaty was sniffing the ground. Pierre pulled the T-shirt over his head and hung it on the back of his neck so his whole chest was exposed to me. I unzipped his shorts and, when they fell to his feet, some coins rolled away. His ticket stuck out of his pocket. It was wrinkled and damp—I had a sudden flash of Pierre during the journey, clutching it tightly inside a sweaty fist. He went down on his knees before me, pushed his head under my T-shirt and pressed his burning tongue to my skin. He slipped his right hand inside and began pulling at the hair on my chest as if trying to rip it right out—Pierre always believed every part of my body belonged to him. He was trying to unbutton my shorts with his other hand when all of a sudden the pungent smell of the dog market filled the house. I let go of Pierre's soft hair and held my hand over my nose, and Pierre started gasping, trying not to inhale, as if he was in a bucket of water. Souriaty was standing next to a yellow pool of urine and faeces, looking back and forth between us. Pierre and I looked at each other and burst out laughing. Pierre wanted to clean it up straight away but I grabbed his arm and threw him on the bed. The squealing bedsprings terrified Souriaty and she curled up under the table, observing us closely through the glass. I finished Pierre's task for him and opened the stubborn buttons, then flung myself on top of him.

The idea behind living in this remote neighbourhood a few kilometres south of Damascus was that Pierre, Souriaty, and I could enjoy a little security. Pierre and I did everything we could to be close to each other. Pierre was the first boy for whom I felt total love, consonance of feeling, humility of soul, and reassurance of spirit. On our double pillow we dreamed that the revolution would be victorious and our relationship would no longer have to be silent, concealed behind curtains. We dreamed much and often and lived out the happiest of days in our private bubble, until it was popped by an explosion at the Palestine branch of the Mukhabarat just a couple of kilometres away—the largest blast in the history of Damascus. From that day, danger crept even into our cramped neighbourhood. One day, Pierre bought a wooden crucifix from the local market and hung it on the door of our flat. He told me that his mother had done the same thing on their house in Aleppo after the Orthodox Church told her that the Assadist army would never raid Christian houses. Pierre didn't trust the church's assertion any more than he believed in the efficacy of his mother's actions but he wanted to protect me and Souriaty in any way he could.

One evening, Pierre, Souriaty and I were on the bed, watching through the open window as a helicopter dropped bombs on the nearby village of Malihah. Behind us, Syrian state television was showing a vixen suckling a baby monkey when suddenly both fox and monkey tumbled into darkness. The electricity had been cut off. Darkness and quiet, pierced by the sound of the distant helicopter. Pierre kissed me firmly then closed the window without locking it. The sound of the helicopter disappeared. I lay on my back and hugged Souriaty to my stomach—she was alarmed when it began rumbling but then she started to lick it with her warm tongue. Pierre lay down next to me and rested his head on my shoulder. The gauzy curtain cast a shadow over our naked bodies, which began wrestling while the darkness in the apartment loomed ominously above us.

A gunshot rang out in the distance. Several men could be heard shuffling outside. More gunfire, heavier this time. Footsteps running on gravel, getting louder as they reached our window. A car engine started up. "Stop the car, you bastard," someone shouted after another gunshot. A baby's wail came from a neighbouring building and was instantly smothered. Pierre got down on the ground and lay on his back. His hand stroked the cross tattooed on his chest as if he were praying. More heavy footsteps beat the ground. I got down and lay next to him, and together we hugged Souriaty. Something exploded close by—the force of it blew the window open and a light hail of gravel rained in, clattering onto the glass tabletop and the ground. There was a fight happening in our narrow street. We stayed where we were. Another intense explosion, followed by running and a manic burst of gunfire. Sudden quiet. The sound of heavy footsteps came again and increased until it stopped right outside our window. One person, apparently kicking something heavy, said, "Is this one dead?" Who was dead? Had Pierre hung himself on his crucifix? I was frozen. An unknown man was dead. He was lying next to us, only an open window away. "Grab that fucking cunt's feet," the same man said in a commanding tone then kicked the corpse hard. The sound of the victim's scalp scraping along the gravel infiltrated every pore of my skin. A car engine. Conversation that couldn't be made out. The car moving further away. Silence.

Later that night we were woken by the echo of bullets hitting the wall of our building. With Souriaty in my arms, I crawled to the bathroom over the gravel still scattered on the floor. Pierre followed. As soon as we closed the bathroom door, a bullet shattered the bathroom's small square window and landed in the wall. We went back into the other room. Souriaty squirmed out of my hands and disappeared under the wardrobe. The gunfire intensified. From the sound of boots outside, it seemed as though an entire battalion was out there. We were a single clot of terror, Pierre, Souriaty, and I, and together we rolled under the bed, twined around each other like barbed wire. My lips accidentally met Pierre's and we clung to each other. I enveloped him from behind and embraced his crucifix, which trembled in my arms. A few grains of gravel were stuck to it. I passed my beard softly over his neck. I breathed slowly into his ear. I nibbled his left earlobe. His body gradually stopped jerking. He took my hand and drew it under his head as a pillow, and he kept my other hand on his chest. His back clung to my chest, and he shifted until the hollows of his body were filled with the swells of mine. The sound of bullets didn't let up, and we didn't stop loving until we trembled from pleasure and warm fluid spilled over our legs, and we fell asleep under the bed.

Ever since the fighting had reached our neighbourhood we had stopped taking Souriaty to the end of the street to do her business, and every morning the stink coming from one corner of the room was like an alarm clock. She, too, demanded freedom; freedom, for her, meant shitting wherever she liked. That morning, sweaty and sluggish, our bodies slid out from beneath the bed like we were crawling out of the crater of an explosion. I opened the window to air the room, pretending that the previous night had been nothing more than a nightmare that could now be forgotten. Something needle-sharp jabbed into the bottom of my foot. Pierre put on his shorts but I flung mine over my head so that they dangled over my shoulders like a thick pair of braids. "How I love mornings with you," Pierre said. I blew him a kiss. He caught it on the tip of his finger and brought it to his heart, then began cleaning the floor. I sat on the edge of the bed, trying to extract the pebble from my foot with my fingernails while Souriaty craned her head to watch me with mournful eyes from beneath the wardrobe. I finally managed to pull it out and threw it into the water, then I picked up my phone and walked on tiptoe, my shorts still covering my head. As I sat on the toilet, Souriaty joined me. She rested her wet belly on the top of my foot and raised her head to rub her neck against me.

We have turned into newspaper pages. We pass every night in printing presses, iron letters ramming words of war and death into our eyes, noses, mouths, asses, and ears. They stick pictures of our faces on dead and rotting bodies. Every morning they hang us like slaughtered animals on the world's kiosks for inspection, twenty-four hours a day, while the next editions are being prepared.

My moment of quiet was interrupted by the sound of boots kicking in the building's outer door. Souriaty darted away. I deleted a video of the helicopter from my phone, along with a video of Pierre and I kissing. I had intended to send it to our friend Sebastián in Spain so he could upload it to YouTube. No one knocked on a door like that apart from the shabiha or the military police. I whipped my shorts off my head and pulled them on as I hurried out of the bathroom. "Call my older brother if they take me," I whispered to Pierre and pushed him away from the entrance. When I opened the door to the apartment, Souriaty ran up behind me. "Open the door, you bastard," yelled one of dozens of men on the other side of the grille. As soon as I did, more than twenty shabiha men streamed inside and up the stairs, ignoring me.

Souriaty was scurrying in among their boots as I tried to pick her up. "Watch out for the puppy, sir—there's a little puppy on the ground there, sir," one of the men pointed out to his commanding officer, a tall, lean man in a loose-fitting military uniform, his top buttons opened to reveal a brown triangle the sun had stamped on his chest. He took Souriaty out of my arms and said, "Nice dog," as he tried to stick his finger, skinny as a prong, in her mouth. "We want a copy of the key to the building. We need to put a sniper on the roof," he went on, as Souriaty tried to wriggle away from him, gazing at me. They wanted to take the violence in the neighbourhood to the third floor and install a murderer there. "What do you want this dog for? It seems like a lot of work—*What's happening up there, you bastards?*" he shouted up the stairs. A stream of shabiha flowed down the stairs. "Sir, everything is just right, it's the best location," one of them said confidently. "If he doesn't have another key, shoot the lock," the commander said, jabbing a thumb at me. He stuffed Souriaty inside his jacket and left as if he had done nothing at all. He had arrested Souriaty. He buried her in his uniform. Conscripted her before knowing her name. One of the shabiha pushed me off the step back inside the apartment and slammed my own door in my face. Pierre pressed his gleaming cross to my cold back and hung me on it. A single shot rang out, destroying the lock.

In our country, we are utterly powerless.

Souriaty's kidnap opened the first rupture between my feet and the earth of my homeland. Immediately Pierre and I resolved to leave the apartment. We packed our bags and left before the water had dried on the ground. Pierre left his wooden crucifix on the door. We headed to the house of my aunt, the famous broadcaster Salma, in the Abu Rummaneh district. I only relied on this aunt in times of real crisis. She understood everything without me having to say a word. She adored Pierre and in his hearing would often repeat that he was precious to her because he was precious to me. We didn't just leave the apartment, we fled from it—not out of fear, but out of despair. We hadn't realised Souriaty's place in our hearts and lives until they took her away. The apartment had become cold, empty, and cramped as if those warm days had never taken place there. Souriaty, our little daughter ... kidnapped right in front of us, and we didn't have the courage to say no. Pierre and I were silent in the taxi to my aunt's house. The car jolted us and the ornament the driver had hung from the roof while the speakers blared music, old songs that glorified Hafez Assad, the Father Dictator. We left Jaramana and entered Damascus where the number of soldiers equalled the number of civilians, perhaps even exceeded them. We stopped at a checkpoint at every square and junction. Some of them asked for our ID cards, others just stared. Damascus had never presented herself like this to me before, cold and unfeeling despite the brilliant sunshine; she was a stranger who didn't recognise me any more than I recognised her. I was looking around in the hope of seeing someone I knew, but everyone, everything, seemed unfamiliar. We reached my aunt Salma's neighbourhood, where there were no soldiers or checkpoints, not even a person on the streets—just eucalyptus trees with dense green leaves that had a jaunty air, and immaculate sports cars, as if their owners had bought them just for show.

My aunt welcomed us in her spacious salon. In a feathered nightdress, her sleep mask lifted onto her forehead like a headband, she seemed to have just woken from a nap. As long as I had known her I had believed she lived in her own private world, insulated from everything that went on in Syria and perhaps the rest of the world too. When Pierre and I refused coffee, she called her maid and asked her to prepare the aubergine kebabs that Pierre loved. She sat down to watch the news bulletin showing the protests in downtown Damascus and began cursing, declaring that anyone who went out to protest must be an anarchist.

She didn't invite me and Pierre to sleep together and asked one of us to sleep in a different room, even though the rooms in her apartment were large and one would have accommodated us both comfortably. In a low voice tinged with sorrow she said, "It's for the best." I didn't understand exactly what she meant. Was it that she wanted me to get used to being away from Pierre or could she not bear to see me in bed with a man?

After midnight, Pierre crept stealthily into my room and found me lying on top of the blanket in the same clothes—I hadn't even removed my shoes. He too hadn't changed since fleeing our apartment and he was in tears. Without a word he lay down next to me. We didn't sleep. We spent the whole night with our eyes locked on the ceiling.

The following day, I had a farewell coffee with Pierre at the In House Café in Shaalan. I gazed at his face; there were tears on his cheeks, as well as a broad loving smile. He reached an open palm towards me, and we clasped hands. He squeezed my hand and rubbed his fingers on my palm as if he wanted something of my skin to be left in his. He lifted my hand to his face and inhaled deeply, holding his breath for a second. Then he closed his eyes and let out a long, slow exhale. Before he left the café and Damascus itself he made me swear, in the name of love, to leave the country.

My face had disappeared in the window glass of the bus back to Åseda. My features became lost in my breath and the breath of the other passengers. I traced a heart in the opaque cloud with the tip of my finger then closed the heart shape left open at the tip. I took my phone and pressed "record"—but my phone died at that very moment. I would close my eyes and pretend to sleep, just like everyone else.

CHAPTER 4

The Secret Revolution

They had bound my wrists tightly behind my back.
The rough cord almost cut off my hands. A man was
pulling my arms up behind my back. He grabbed my
neck roughly and pushed me downwards. Using a
strip of foul-smelling fabric, they bound my eyes so
I couldn't see a thing.

I only heard their voices whisper to each other,
"This fag should be killed."

My body trembled, and beads of sweat slid from
my brow. I had thought I was on familiar terms with
terror, but I only learned its true nature in the instant
I found myself standing on a ledge. My body was
buffeted by a strong wind, and I almost fell into the
empty space in front of me.

"Push him off, throw this kafir off. Filthy sodomite."

These words, mingled with foul breath, crashed
into me. A warm arm wound around my neck like a
noose and choked me. Rough hands made sure the
rope around my wrists was tight. A foot kicked the
middle of my back. I fell into nothingness.

I woke in a panic. My eyes were straining open but
I couldn't see a thing. Blackness. Ragged breathing, a
sense of suffocation. I put my hands to my face and
realised it was the sleeping mask I'd forgotten I'd put
on. I lifted it from my eyes. It was daytime now. I was

submerged in a sea of sweat on the narrow bed where I had slept ever since my arrival to the asylum seekers' building in Åseda.

A strong smell of nicotine wafted in from beneath the door. Outside, men's voices were coming from the kitchen. I felt sick. I groped under the bed for my phone and saw it was ten in the morning. In need of coffee, I walked cautiously towards the kitchen and was hit with a thick cloud of smoke when I opened the door. My flatmates were hosting their friends from the next apartment, and all of them were sitting around the table talking rowdily in various Arabic dialects, cigarettes dancing between their lips and fingers.

I tried to smile but failed. They were discussing the latest news—how Daesh had imposed authority on several schools in the areas of northern Syria under their control.

"Coffee's ready," my flatmate Abu Adnan told me, stirring the coffee as it bubbled in the rakwa.

"What kind of education are these criminals giving our kids?" said one of the men, stubbing out his cigarette in the ashtray in front of him.

Another added, "Assad's regime murdered our children, and Daesh is turning them into extremists."

I was listening to them, my body still twitching from the nightmare that had woken me. I interrupted them, "Daesh are killing anyone who disagrees with them: women without a niqab, men who don't support them. They rape women and throw gay people off buildings. Haven't you seen their videos?"

"You mean fags? Ugh, perverts," another man said, lighting a new cigarette with the stub of his old one.

The others nodded in agreement. One, the man who had said how worried he was that Daesh was controlling children, said, "The Qur'an says they're sinners. Sodomites! We never heard of any of this till we came to Sweden. This sin is a disease that asylum seekers catch in Europe."

I realised the nightmare I had woken from was still ongoing and very real—it was being enacted around the kitchen table. When I looked at the men, how they smoked and talked, smoked and talked, their heads seemed like chimneys puffing out noxious black smoke. I couldn't stay there. My tongue stuck to the roof of my mouth. Did I have to keep silent, even in Sweden?

I went back to my room in defeat. When I sat on my bed, a profound sense of emptiness rolled over me, but I decided to resist the loneliness and sadness that had become my daily companions. Having already filled the journal I had bought to record my life in Åseda, and having to wait until my asylum seeker's allowance arrived at the end of the month to buy a new one, I hung onto every bit of paper that came my way. I even began scribbling on the backs of the letters that came from the Immigration Bureau. That day I picked up one of their envelopes and slid out an old letter inviting me to an official meeting to claim asylum. As usual, I wavered between using English or Arabic to express the thoughts about my present and my past that whirled around me. I took a deep breath to prepare myself and summon up what I wanted to say this time; afterwards, all I found myself writing was reportage about some of the places that had helped me know and come to terms with myself.

In the asylum-seekers' building I usually wrote in English; I felt that this language would be more helpful in hiding what I wrote, given that my flatmates could not read it.

From now on, it won't be kept secret. I read once there will never be true change until we own our bodies, and we have to fight for that. I have to tell people about this invisible world which has been growing underground for so long.

Sibky Park

Every Saturday, families flocked to Sibky Park in the Shaalan neighbourhood in central Damascus. Shaalan still bore traces of its colonial past, boasting large palaces that provided abundant housing for a range of nationalities: French, Italian, Greek, Russian, and Armenian. It was a mix of Muslims and Christians who lived side by side. Sibky Park was at the intersection of Shaalan Street and Hafez Ibrahim Street, close to a busy market that sold fruit, vegetables, and pirated cassettes of the latest Western pop music. Certain Damascenes considered it perfect for cruising. The avenue, lined on either side with palm trees, was well known to gay men who came there from all parts of the country.

My first visit to Sibky Park took place one October evening in 2000, just after I turned nineteen. I knew its reputation thanks to my classmates at school—whenever they wanted to throw out an insult, they'd say *Go fuck a guy in Sibky Park.*

I was greeted at the gate by a man in his thirties who

sported an awe-inspiring moustache. He was wearing a black leather jacket and grey cotton trousers that were tight over his thighs and effortlessly showed off the bulge in his crotch. His name was Essam. I had met him a week earlier in his clothes shop in Shaalan. When he suggested a few shirts that might suit me, I had liked his kind manner and the way he gently touched my shoulders and back. I felt we had something in common, although we didn't say much to each other. He suggested meeting in Sibky Park the following week and gave me his business card. After a few days I decided to accept his invitation.

After we said hello, his first words to me before we had even left the gate were, "The secret police are watching this place. Most people know that gay men come here to meet, but they don't stop us as long as we don't cause any problems."

I heard this with a mixture of anxiety and excitement. At last he looked straight at me and admitted, "The secret police don't like us because we rebel against the law and we're used to going after what we want."

I asked him how we could be arrested if we were just two men walking in a park. He said, "They'll accuse you of anything to put you in jail. Honestly, the official accusations are a relief because at least they don't create scandal. Even so, the police will threaten to tell your family you're a pervert who has the kind of sex that enrages God and society—unless you pay them to keep quiet."

I was terrified at the thought of bringing shame on my family. I was afraid that Essam himself belonged to the secret police, and he was the one who would seize me. Without a word, I left him and walked out of the park.

There is a saying in Arabic: *Everything forbidden is desired.* Essam's use of the word *rebel* fascinated me, and I was drawn back to Sibky Park later that week. On that second visit I met Essam by chance; he seemed more relaxed this time, and I felt more at ease around him. The park seemed green and clean although a few lamps were broken, throwing some areas into shadow. The middle of the park featured a rectangular pond with a water fountain, making it an attractive place for a stroll. I could see a couple of street hawkers selling corn, cigarettes, and newspapers and, in the back of the park, a young woman playing with her infant child.

Essam told me that gay men began to congregate here from 8 pm. Usually the older man would sit on the benches around the pond while the younger men chose the banks on the main walkway. He said I could choose where to sit according to the kind of men I liked. All communication was done with the eyes— you focused your gaze on the person you were attracted to, followed by a smile. If they responded in kind, you had to walk with them to the public toilets. Once inside, there might be an intimate meeting or just a kiss. There was no privacy either way.

When we were near the bathrooms, Essam advised me to keep a constant watch on the door. He said, "It's very, very dangerous, but it's delicious."

The place stank and I couldn't bring myself to kiss anyone in such a filthy place, especially when the old defunct copper taps dripped into a pool that could have been water or urine—not to mention the panic that gripped me. Fear and nausea killed all my sexual desire, and I ran out of the bathroom before Essam got anywhere near me. From my reaction, Essam understood that the toilets of Sibky Park wouldn't suit me. He followed and found me standing by the main gate outside the park, trembling. Apparently, my fear and bewilderment were plain to see. He offered me a cigarette, and I snatched it from him with a shaking hand—I wanted smoke to scrub the lingering stink of shit and piss from my nostrils and throat. As he lit my cigarette Essam said, "There are other places to meet men. Havens that are safe and clean— in fact, you'll leave cleaner than when you went in. The hammams ... the hammams of Damascus."

I was floored when Essam leaned in close to describe them to me in a whisper, his breath tickling my earlobe.

"They're full of naked men hidden by steam, so you don't see what they're doing, you only feel it. Their moans and cries slide into your hearing and your vision begins to clear, little by little, until the flesh you're running your fingers over emerges, and you can make out the silhouettes of the men attached to each other. You won't smell anything but laurel soap, and the only thing running over your bare feet will be jets of warm water inviting you to get on your knees and join in."

Hammam Amouna

On a narrow street in the Amara district in the old city, Hammam Amouna was concealed from the eyes of passersby behind a door. The only people who knew about it were those who knew where they were going or had been guided there. Back in Ottoman times, Amouna had been a common woman's name, and I once heard from one of the other patrons that the hammam had been named after its owner. She had designated it as a place solely for women, where they could learn about their bodies and their desires—a place where they could do and say whatever they wanted. The hammam had retained its name but eventually became a haven for men who tossed their secrets into each other's bodies, then left less heavy and less silent.

The entrance to the hammam was a small wooden door that opened wide, adorned by a slack curtain for privacy. The hammam seemed to be about a metre below ground, hidden beneath an arch close to the Grand Mosque such that its minaret also adjoined the hammam building. On my first visit I took a deep breath before I raised the curtain, went down five steps, and entered. I was welcomed by a man sitting behind a large wooden table that held a landline telephone, a radio, and a selection of folded towels. The man, who was in his thirties, seemed nice; he had a round face with a smooth chin, a moustache, and short curly hair. When he said, "Hello, little kitty," his kindness was only confirmed for me. I handed over my wallet as Essam had instructed me, and he put it in a little drawer, locked it, and handed me the key hanging from a rubber bracelet. He gave me a towel from the pile in front of him and invited me to take off my clothes and hang them on one of the pegs on the wall.

I was the only patron in the barrany. The place seemed small and humble, not at all what I had imagined. It was lit by a single lamp that swung from the ceiling. The taps of the fountain in the centre of the room were shut off, but the fountain basin was filled with water. Rose petals floated on its surface. On the edge of the fountain was a brazier with live coals which I guessed were for shisha pipes, and beside it I saw some earthenware pots holding basil plants. Clothes pegs occupied the walls which were covered in men's trousers, jeans, shirts, and coats, all in black and grey. Black leather shoes were scattered over the ground, cracked and worn-out—their owners appeared to use them as sandals by folding down the heels. Balls of socks were stuffed into their toes.

I didn't find it easy to undress. I hesitated but eventually managed to wrap a cotton towel—whose original white had turned beige from use—around my waist. My heart was racing. Two young-looking men I guessed were hammam workers came out from one of the doors, and when they spotted a shy young man hovering uncertainly, they smiled at me and then at each other. One of them came up and handed me a roll of loofah with a piece of laurel soap inside, introducing himself as Maher the masseur. His words, his mild manner, and the touch of his hand as he gave me the loofah all eased my anxiety and made me keen to enter this "haven," as Essam had called it. My body quivered in anticipation of what might be awaiting me. I went through the same door the workers had come out of and found myself in a small room which would have been entirely dark if not for the faint light from the small glass apertures in the ceiling. The toilets on the right emitted a foul smell, so I kept going until I reached a miniscule room with a door in each corner. A group of bare-chested, bearded men were sitting on a wooden bench and they had the same towels wrapped around their waists. I felt their gazes on my bare chest and, embarrassed, I hurried on to the jawany. I felt myself tumble into a warm pool of steam. Despite the dense cloud, I made out a group of men standing in the middle of the room. I was too shy to invite someone with my eyes, so I looked up at the ceiling, another large dome filled with glass holes to let in the daylight.

I lowered my gaze again and pushed deeper into the vapours. The hot water taps were open some-where, running over the ground and tickling my feet. I could see two cubicles facing each other. There were no doors but each was closed off by a curtain and had a man standing outside seeming to keep watch. I put myself in the corner next to a tap and sat on the ground where I could peek under a towel that had been hung over the entrance to one of the cubicles. I could see two pairs of thick, hairy legs moving. Soon, one of the men knelt down, and the other remained standing. As I watched, I could barely contain the feeling building in my crotch. I was torn between my desire to enter and see what they were doing, and panic at seeing all of this happen in public. Suddenly, out of nowhere, a moustachioed man appeared in front of me and said, "Is this your first time here?"

I nodded and glanced shyly at his body. His skin was white and unusually soft-looking, and he seemed to be in his forties. I noticed the odd way he wrapped his towel around his full waist, as though it was a miniskirt. "My name is Sahar," he said, pointing to the tattoo on his left shoulder. I was surprised to see his name, a female one, tattooed there in Latin letters but without vowels, so it read: SHR. He asked me if I wanted to address him as a girl, and I said I would prefer not to. He burst out laughing and said, "That's what you all say on your first visit." He gazed into my face with wide eyes. "Then once you relax you all ask if you can call me 'she.' Anyway, it's better to be a stallion in this damn society ... Be a top, it's not easy being Sahar."

He concluded by cupping his tits and wiggling his shoulders. He came so close to me that I could feel his breath, warmer even than the rest of the room.

"Abu Emad wants to have sex with you in one of these little rooms. Say yes and you won't regret it."

He jiggled his chest in my face, and I felt the blood congeal in my veins as I imagined myself in the place of those two men, of whom I could see only bare feet and hairy legs. Sahar poured cold water over my head and said again, "Do you want Abu Emad or what? He's in a hurry."

I was curious to see Abu Emad—what he looked like, how old he was. I said yes.

Abu Emad turned out to be in his early thirties, with a broad-set body and hairy chest. He had a beard and short, thick, black hair. He looked like the traditional men from Rif Dimashq, and my suspicions were soon confirmed when he told me he was from Douma, about half an hour from downtown Damascus. He offered me a local brand of cigarette and when I refused, he nodded approvingly and said I had passed the first test. He preferred a clean mouth which didn't stink of smoke. He told me he was a taxi driver, and he was married with a five-year-old kid. I found it strange that he was telling me all these details when we were there to have sex, but I kept quiet. Then he asked if I minded if he went to pray in the barrany. He apologised, explaining that he didn't want to miss Maghrib prayer before it went dark. He left me alone and utterly bewildered.

Why all this information? Had he left so suddenly because he didn't like me? Or was he only trying to find out whether I was gay so he could come back with other men to arrest me?

The walls of the hammam began to close in around me and the temperature rose.

Within a few minutes, Abu Emad reappeared with a mischievous grin and asked me to follow him into one of the cubicles. When we went inside he took the towel from around his waist and hung it on the door, before inviting me to do the same.

I went back to Amouna several times after that and soon realised that Abu Emad wasn't the only married man there. Even Sahar had a wife and kids. There were young guys who came to Amouna to have sex for the first time; those from a conservative background couldn't sleep with women before marriage. Some of them kept visiting Amouna even after they were married; some never came back. I loved meeting other gay men to talk and share the experiences we'd had with our families, in our communities. I found friendship there. The sex I preferred was with men who thought of themselves as straight. Every time I visited Amouna I felt at home and soon stopped caring about the dirt. Every time, I discovered something new within myself. I grew used to being naked and I loved my body more; I was no longer shy, or ashamed of any part of it. Whenever I left the hammam I felt lighter and my body felt freer—I would fly along the narrow alleys of the old medina, wanting to sing and leap for joy. It was enough, the certainty that I wasn't alone in the world. There were others like me. I loved being a man and loving other men, so much that every time I had sex, I thanked God for granting me this desire and making me this way.

Hammam Qaymariya

Hammam Amouna wasn't the only hammam, but it was my first. In my early years in Damascus, a visit to the hammam every Friday at prayer-time became obligatory. In my opinion, it was the safest time to go to the hammams as the streets were almost empty. And additionally, there were hordes of men, especially married men, who found it a perfect excuse for leaving their families.

Getting naked in front of unknown men in the galleries and compartments of the hammam gave me increasing confidence and power. Soon I was naked the whole time, walking among the other men and chatting, completely forgetting that not a shred of fabric covered any part of my body.

Like thousands of others, tourists and locals alike, I used to enjoy visiting Qaymariya in the evening when the hammam was open for men. Qaymariya was a neighbourhood famed for its ancient character, authentic food, and the old shisha cafés whose reputations went back generations, such as Naufara Café. Whenever I walked through its stone archways on my way to buy some new CDs from my favourite record shop, I would inhale the scent of the jasmine that had taken root in the walls. One evening in 2003 I saw a blue sign on a stone wall that read *Hammam Qaymariya* and, below it, a group of young guys chatting. I couldn't help smiling and feeling a connection with them—I left Hammam Amouna feeling exactly the same way.

Without another thought, I changed my trajectory and went inside. The entrance fee was 150 liras, double the price of Amouna. I wasn't too concerned about the difference, however; I had already noticed the stark difference between the two hammams.

In Hammam Qaymariya, the barrany was lit by a copper lamp in the shape of a hand from which coloured glass swung. The floor was smooth marble and the walls were old stone but they had been restored and varnished. As for the fountain, it was the size of a small swimming pool, and it had a copper tap in the shape of a lion with a water jet coming out of its open mouth. What particularly caught my eye were the ropes hanging from the ceiling on which dozens of colourful towels had been spread like flags.

A member of staff welcomed me warmly and said I was in luck; the hammam was reserved for women until 6 pm, so I had arrived at the time appointed for men. One of them asked me if it was my first time in a public hammam. When I replied that I was a patron of Hammam Amouna, he smiled broadly, patted my shoulder, and promised I would enjoy what I saw inside.

In Hammam Qaymariya, the clientele were different too. Here, I got to know doctors, engineers, lawyers, and many tourists, both Arabs and foreigners. The owners and workers at the hammam were more relaxed and occasionally, if the mood was right, they would turn off the lights so they could join in and play with us in secret. On those occasions, the place became like a dark room, and I and dozens of other men would become one mass of intertwining bodies sharing frenzied sexual encounters. Hamma Qaymariya was very special. Sometimes we came across items the women had left behind, such as combs, hair clips, and scarves—even bras—and we would try them on, giggling.

A few years later, I met a gorgeous Iraqi man in this hammam. He told me that he had emigrated to Sweden in 2005 and lived in Malmö, but he came to Damascus to meet his family, who were now refugees living in Syria. I was very keen to know more about the life of gay men in Sweden and took him to sit down with me on a marble sofa in the jawany. He admitted that gay life in Sweden wasn't as exciting as in Damascus, which surprised me; I had always thought of Sweden as a country where gay men could be open about their sexuality.

He said, "Hammam Qaymariya is a great place to meet men. Look around—there are dozens of men here, and it's only Tuesday. Everyone's relaxed and talking to each other. It's impossible to find anywhere like this in Sweden, even on the weekend." He smiled at the doubt that appeared on my face and went on, "Gay saunas barely exist over there."

He acknowledged he was lucky to have ended up in

Sweden after the devastation of Iraq, particularly in Malmö, where he could easily travel to Copenhagen to visit Amigo Sauna. I sneaked glances at his body, which was muscly and well-proportioned. He told me that very few gay Swedes were interested in Arab men.

"Perhaps they're afraid of us because we're foreigners. But in my experience, most of them just see me as a sex toy ... that's all they want to do with me. They pick me up in a club and the next morning I have to go—they don't even offer me a cup of coffee. Even if we had a great time in bed or at the bar, if I meet them in the street a few days later they ignore me completely. On the other hand," he remarked, "some Arabic or Middle Eastern men don't like sleeping with Swedes. They don't like men who are uncircumcised. They think it's unclean, and they're not used to dicks looking like that."

I asked him if it was safe for an Arab to be gay in Sweden.

"Many of them are afraid to come out because they live with their families in the suburbs. They still feel ashamed and unsafe."

After a pause he asked me to stop the interrogation—he felt like he was being interviewed for a political talk show. Instead he told me about his favourite sauna in Copenhagen, Amigo Sauna, which held several darkrooms and separate spaces for kinks, including s&m, along with a cinema room showing porn. I was very taken with his description.

During the summer in Damascus the hammams were half-empty, and gay men went there only rarely. Instead they preferred to spend time in the parks, squares, and swimming pools. On warm nights gay activity increased in public places like Hamra Street in Shaalan. This area first sprang into life during a period of renewal in the forties and fifties. Its origins were strongly linked with the colonial period of the French Mandate and local resistance to the League of Nations' idea that Syria wasn't ready for full independence. Several shops opened there during this period so that Western and imported products could be found for sale in among the carpenters, the metal furniture shops, and the falafel makers. This street was crammed with shoppers and traders during the day—and the field was cleared for a different group of visitors after nightfall.

Some would cruise back and forth along Hamra in their cars while others would walk on the pavements beneath the streetlights, avidly watching for any gesture that indicated desire for an encounter. Stopping was dangerous as the police could raid the place at any time, so everyone kept moving normally, observing the bodies of others, and subtly displaying their own for those in the shadows. There was nowhere to have sex in the streets or backstreets—here, there was merely communication through glances and smiles. Matters culminated in a conversation inside someone's car or in front of one of the shops, then we would go to someone's home or to the hammam.

My aunt Salma lived in the heart of this neighbour-hood in Shaalan. One night in 2003, after I had visited her, I decided to return home through Shaalan and Hamra Street in the hope of meeting someone on the way. While I was walking, a taxi pulled up next to me and two men got out. One of them came up to me and reached out as if he wanted to shake my hand. When I raised mine in response, he suddenly slapped hand-cuffs around my wrist and pushed me inside the car. They took my identity card and began to insult me, calling me a filthy pervert and saying I loved cock more than my mother and sister. I had never received such abuse in my life and I burst into tears. They con-tinued their humiliation, and their words made bile rise in my stomach. One of the policemen slapped me on my neck from behind while the other one said, "What are you doing here?"

"I was visiting my aunt."

"Is your aunt a whore like you?" the other one asked.

I couldn't move—they were restraining my shoul-ders. I told them my aunt was a broadcaster and gave her full name.

I begged them, "You can call her."

They fell silent and stopped the car. One of them ordered the other to return my ID card and let me go. As soon as they did, I ran home and looked at the bleeding wounds around my wrist. I wondered what would have happened if my aunt had been a regular person.

I spent the following week inside the house, terri-fied that someone might notice the wounds the cuffs had left on my wrist. I didn't go outside once, not even to university. Every time the landline rang, my heart would race. I remembered what someone had said once in Amouna. "The hammams are safe because it's normal to find naked men there; there's nothing to arouse suspicion."

In December 2005 I saw a news article that said the government had closed down Hammam Amouna; the reason given was that the building was decrepit and liable to collapse. But when I ran into Sahar in the street, he told me that the morality police had raided the building and arrested the owners and attendants who were inside after someone informed on them.

"I was lucky—I wasn't there that day," he said.

It was the first time I had met Sahar on the street in all these years. At first I hardly recognised him in his shabby clothes; I was used to seeing him glistening and smooth and naked in the hammams.

"But there's an interesting place, similar atmosphere to Amouna, where handsome men with no money go when they want to fuck—try Biblos Cinema."

At this, Sahar disappeared into the crowded street.

Telephone Conversation With My Assigned Caseworker

Sitting on my small bed in the asylum seekers' building in Åseda and recording my past made me feel like a flying carpet was taking me back to the streets of Damascus. I could smell the herbs and spices of the souks, I could hear the conversation of the men in the hammams, and I could feel the hot steam on my body. I thought to myself: *Those poor men, sitting and smoking in the kitchen—they don't know a thing about pleasure, they don't know a thing about life, maybe they don't know anything at all—and they don't even realise it.*

I had met people like them before but I had never been forced to live with them. It was frightening. I always considered them simply uninformed, victims of ignorance. I wondered how I could convince them that being gay is special, and not a sin? I picked up my phone and walked over to the window overlooking the graveyard. I called my caseworker and asked her whether she had any update, three months after my asylum request had been submitted.

"No news, unfortunately," she said apologetically. I asked her whether she knew that Daesh had sentenced a homosexual man to be thrown off a tall building before being stoned to death?

No, she didn't know. And she didn't know about all the young men who had been murdered in secret by Assad's regime because they had refused to join his army. I wanted to tell her it wasn't easy to live and share a space with men who openly ridiculed gay men, but I didn't want to cause them any harm—they too were victims, of ignorance and dictatorship. I ended the conversation and closed the curtain; I didn't want to see the graveyard, I didn't want to think about death. I had come to Sweden to escape the horrors I had been subjected to over the last few years and here I was, facing the same thing, forced to remain in a remote forest and cut off from humanity. I returned to my notebook and found the last thing I wrote: *Cinema Biblos.*

Sahar gave me directions: "Walk through Marja Square and head towards Nasr Street. You'll see Sadiq Restaurant on your left. Go straight and you'll find a shop window with a large poster for an old Syrian film. That's Cinema Biblos."

I was on my way: I felt like everyone around me knew where I was going.

I reached the cinema door and paused by the poster for *I Die and Love You Again*, a classic from 1976 starring Ighra, a name associated with erotic scenes and adult-only films. A photo showed her with kohl-lined eyes, looking straight at the camera with a gaze that brimmed over with lust. I regarded her photo, particularly her eyes which held a mixture of vulnerability, desire, and power.

I paid twenty-five liras to a wizened old man in the ticket booth and went inside. The entrance hall was painted a gleaming pink, and the walls were covered in movie posters and photos of Syrian actresses from the seventies in various alluring poses that displayed their thighs and breasts. There were classic Syrian films from the same era with intriguing titles such as *Girls of Summer*, *Dancing on the Wounds*, and *Bride from Damascus*. There was a saying that some Syrians used to repeat whenever they saw photos of Ighra: *Hell needs firewood*. I was desperate to enter Ighra's hell.

In the entrance hall I saw two older men who seemed to be of retirement age, sitting and smoking on the steps going down. One of them had a cane beside him. They smiled at me as I went into the cinema. When I passed them, I wondered when they too fell into hell, this hidden world where, so it seemed, Ighra was the divinity and the sons of her generation were her followers.

I thought of my beloved Ighra saying "I'll make my body a bridge for Syrian cinema to pass over," and was eager to discover more of this place.

It consisted of a single hall with two floors, a ground floor and a mezzanine with additional seating. It was dark, lit only by the flashing light of the screen showing an old black-and-white film. The place was definitely dirtier than Hammam Amouna. The stink of nicotine saturated everything and probably dated back to when the film was made. I left the ground floor with my hand over my mouth—I felt sick. In the vestibule I saw a sign for the bathroom, so I headed there. Once inside, I heard footsteps coming out from one of the cubicles and smelled a truly abhorrent stench. Two men wearing jalabiyas were standing by a broken urinal, apparently inseparable. A third man appeared from the bathroom stall next to them. I felt like they were all waiting for my assent, so I smiled at them as a token of peace. At once, the man who had been hiding in the cubicle sank to his knees while the other two men raised their jalabiyas over their thick, hairy legs, and the kneeling man began sucking both their erect penises at the same time. As for me, I had automatically turned into the doorman.

The threesome was hot, but the revolting smell from the toilets made the nicotine seem almost bearable by comparison, so I returned to the cinema hall. My eyes had adjusted to the dark and I was able to make out groups of men, so I did my best to steal glances at their faces as far as the light from the screen allowed. It seemed as though most were sitting at the end of the hall in silence. The film dialogue was the only sound. I suddenly spotted a pool on the floor reflecting the light from the screen; my nausea rose once again and I decided to go up to the mezzanine. I wandered in among the seats, looking for an empty place—the mezzanine was crowded. I was about to sit down when a hand grabbed my arm, causing me to panic. I felt a cramp in my stomach as if I had been stabbed. When my gaze fell on the hand's owner, I recognised their eyes at once.

"Marhaba. It's Sahar. So you're gracing the Cinema Biblos with your presence?"

He vanished as quickly as he had appeared, and I remained frozen. I wondered why I always ran into him in places gay men frequented, why he wanted to know everyone. He hadn't been in Amouna when it was raided—was that merely coincidence, or was he a double agent?

During the break between films, the lights came on suddenly and blinded me for a few seconds. Then I saw the place clearly for the first time. There were rows and rows of broken-down seats with torn covers. A few young guys in military uniforms were so deeply asleep on them that even the light didn't wake them. The others, the ones standing up, seemed to be peasants in traditional jalabiyas. The forbidden paradise instantly transformed into a seedy ghetto for penniless gay men. A man came in carrying a tray with plastic cups of tea and did his best to sell some. I was disgusted—how could anyone drink tea in a place like this? In this pause, the beat of a dance song was blaring from the ancient speakers in the corners of the room. I could hear Sahar on the lower floor chatting and laughing, so I edged over to the balcony and saw him dancing, shaking his shoulders in the middle of a group of men. At that moment, observing his raucous laughter and his unnaturally exaggerated movements, I couldn't silence my suspicions about him. Who could possibly be this relaxed unless they were supported by security? His eyes landed on me from below—he waved at me, inviting me to join in. I decided to leave.

That wasn't the end, though. I returned to Cinema Biblos a handful of times because it gave me the chance to speak to a type of gay man different to the ones I normally met. Humble men in their seventies spent their evenings congregating there and chatting, and I was curious to know what their life had been like in the fifties and sixties. They told me that Damascus used to be more free; they told me about the apartments they used to rent in order to live with each other and take in anyone who had been thrown out by their families. They told me the story of how Sibky Park became a haven for gay men after some homeless men put on belly dancing shows in women's outfits. I felt increasingly safe in that invisible world, as if we were members of a secret brotherhood. Under the tutelage of these men, I was learning and becoming stronger. Despite being in constant danger, I discovered that I was able to survive.

At the start of the century, the internet began to spread and became widely available to the middle classes in Aleppo and Damascus—and Deir Ezzor. Many young Syrians enthusiastically adopted these new technologies which could be accessed in the cafés that proliferated throughout the country. At the same time, after war broke out in Iraq in 2003, Damascus saw increasing torrents of refugees fleeing a country mired in chaos and sectarianism. Over two million Iraqis came to Syria during this period. Then another wave of refugees came from Lebanon in June 2006. The General Directorate of the Mukhabarat was responsible for observing the movements and intentions of this influx of foreigners. From its previous occupation of hunting homosexuals, the Syrian police turned to grappling with increasing demands for freedom of expression, freedom of assembly, and the right to protest. It was clear that our association with Iraqi and Lebanese people was a source of unease for the Mukhabarat apparatus.

This hub of chaos also affected many people's sex lives. After 2006 numerous entertainment spots opened in Damascus. In the south of the city, Jaramana began to expand with new residents who came from every corner of Syria, in the same way it had once received Iraqi refugees. Jaramana was like a congregation of the working classes: Druze, Arabs, Alawites, Kurds, and Armenians all lived on top of one another in housing compounds. That's just how Jaramana was. It was the place chosen by Syrians who wanted to discreetly marry someone of a different sect; no one seemed to care very much about anyone else's sect or religion there. Its main street was filled with local restaurants, cafés, and clothes shops. Asylum seekers found it a haven due to the low rents. Immigrant Iraqi businessmen opened nightclubs where singers and dancers performed every night. There were posters pasted on every wall, depicting teenage Iraqi girls and boys and announcing live shows. During this time, some took advantage of the turmoil; the owners of Hammam Qaymariya sold up and bought Hammam Jaramana with the aim of making it like Qaymariya and Amouna, feeling that the sex business had begun to grow in Jaramana. Even so, when I visited Hammam Jaramana for the first time, the owners told me to be wary. Many policemen went to Hammam Jaramana to bathe as the area generally lacked water. The policemen who bathed and left would pay a single lira; this enraged the hammam owner but he didn't dare confront them. The hammam was also well known among local residents, and many Iraqi refugees went there, some to bathe, others for sex.

I felt most comfortable having sex with Iraqi refugees because I was convinced they wouldn't be working for the Mukhabarat.

In June 2008, I met a hot Iraqi guy called Mustafa at Hammam Jaramana. He came up to me and asked me in a thick Iraqi accent if I was Syrian. He went on to say he was new in Damascus and wanted to know where he could buy the best bread and halawiyat in Jaramana. I couldn't believe my luck. I tied my towel around my waist like Sahar used to do, as if it was a miniskirt. Then I leaned closer and offered to show him the tastiest delicacies in Jaramana. But Mustafa confessed that he wasn't looking for a man for himself—he wanted to introduce me to his flatmate who was also from Iraq and who liked sleeping with younger guys. After an appropriate session in the hammam which involved only bathing, we left together to meet his roommate. On the way Mustafa told me they both worked as drivers for GMC, transferring refugees from Baghdad to Damascus. They lived in the square at the entrance to Jaramana. Mustafa invited me inside his apartment, which was empty apart from a leather sofa and a pack of plastic water bottles in the corner of the living room.

Mustafa explained the flat was for Iraqi drivers travelling between Damascus and Baghdad who needed somewhere to stay for a night or two, then he excused himself to go to the kitchen to make some drinks. I looked around me. The walls were white and bare, with only a fluorescent lightbulb to light the whole room. I couldn't see any pictures or even a clock. It was very hot and when he turned on the ceiling fan, it moved so lethargically it was practically useless.

A stocky man with a beard came in. He was wearing a beige jalabiya and seemed to have just come out of the shower. His hair was wet. He headed straight for me, greeted me, and told me his name was Alawi. He sat next to me on the sofa and began to fire questions at me: my name, my age, my job. Mustafa came in from the kitchen with a tray holding a water jug with some ice, a bottle of arak, a bowl of yoghurt, and three glasses. He sat on the floor and invited me and Alawi to join him, as it was cooler on the tiles. I tried the arak that Alawi offered me but found it too strong. As time passed, the three of us grew more relaxed and we began to chat about Jaramana, acknowledging it as a special place, not just in Damascus, but in all of Syria. The conversation became more profound with every sip of arak. We spoke about the war, about migration, about their treacherous daily journey.

Mustafa said, "The road between Baghdad and Damascus is like the line separating life and death." Alawi became tearful as he confessed his fear every time he drove his car to Baghdad and his relief whenever he crossed the border back into Syria. At that time, when I hadn't yet experienced war, I found it hard to understand the gravity of his words. We touched on every subject apart from sex, which was the fundamental reason I was visiting Alawi, so I decided to ambush him. By this time Alawi was drunk and he said, "I don't have sex with men—I have sex with girls, and guys who look like girls. If I can't find a woman, a smooth young guy's body does the same job."

Although the evening didn't end as I had hoped, I enjoyed their company and their conversation. I left their apartment at three in the morning, reflecting how I had spoken freely on subjects that would have been taboo with other Syrians.

As time passed, I became good friends with Mustafa and Alawi. I visited them often and met other drivers who stayed there before heading back. The apartment was filled with horny men who longed for a body to embrace and make love to before a long, exhausting journey. They found total relief in my repeated visits to the apartment, which made Alawi, and eventually even Mustafa, invite me into their beds in the end.

Gays Online

The new technology spread quickly throughout Syria despite still being exorbitantly expensive. Smartphones and laptops and 3G eventually became widespread, but in 2007 there were several attempts by the Assad regime to block social networks. Nevertheless, sex sites remained accessible, along with gay networks like Manjam, the global website to meet gay men, which had more than a thousand members in Damascus, and several hundred in the other governorates.

Manjam was my virtual window into the world of gay men from other Arab countries, including Egypt and the Gulf states. I also started chatting with gay men from Europe as I was curious about what it was like there. I was avid to know more about their lives—did they have to profess their sexual leanings at an early age? I wanted to know how gay marriage worked—was it exactly the same as it was for straight people? But I soon realised that the European men I met over the internet couldn't care less about gay rights—they were only interested in me for sex. I was their fantasy of the Oriental man with dark skin and a beard. Once, I was speaking to a man from Austria who said he was looking for an Arab husband to treat like a wife.

Through Manjam I also connected with a Lebanese

man called Fadi who arranged trips to Damascus and Beirut for gay Western tourists. He admitted that Damascus was the first stop for gay tourists from Europe and the USA—they preferred Damascus to Beirut because they thought that Syrian men were more "authentic" than Lebanese men, who were more Western in their appearance.

A few months later Fadi called me to say he was coming to Damascus with a group of tourists from Finland. And soon after that he called from the Hotel Oriental near Bab Touma where they were staying. We arranged to meet in the main square in the medina so I could show them around. We stopped at Naufara, the tourist café close to the Umayyad mosque. Before I met them they had already visited one of the hammams and seemed amazed by the sheer quantity of gay men there. It apparently hadn't occurred to them that it was the only place where gay men in Syria could meet and be their true selves. There were no gay clubs or bars but a very small number accepted us, such as Disco Saray, Bar Marmar, and El Matador, all in the medina. There, we could meet other men, but we still had to keep an eye out for danger.

One night I took them to Bar Marmar to show them how a bar could welcome gay men without flying a rainbow flag over the door. It was movie night and they were showing *Dreamgirls*, and after the film there was a DJ. We drank and danced till 3 am. On the way back to the hotel, we wandered through the ancient, narrow streets. I remember that night well despite the alcohol, and I also remember how I told them, "I am so glad I was born in Syria and get to be young in Damascus, no matter the fear and danger. I love Damascus even if she is cruel to me."

Underground Revolution

The battle wasn't over yet. It seemed if you were gay and Syrian, you always had to fight for your rights, even in Sweden. In Syria, I had hidden my sexuality from my closest friends, even during the war. I had been afraid of prison, of losing my job, of losing my social life, afraid of being rejected. I preferred to hide who I was in exchange for acceptance and friendship, but I felt humiliated and ashamed by my silence.

I remembered how every moment of persecution had given me strength and courage. I thought of the school pupils in Daraa who started the Syrian revolution in March 2011 by writing slogans about freedom on the walls of their school.

Yet here I was in the asylum seekers' building in Åseda. In a place of safety—apparently. If I didn't begin my own revolution, no one would ever notice I existed.

Early the next morning, when everyone in the building was in bed, I closed my journal and took my pen to the laundry room in the basement. I began writing on the walls.

> *Gay people have rights here.*
> *Gay people are human like you.*
> *Being gay is a sexual orientation, not a disease.*
> *Even if you don't accept gay people, don't attack them.*

Gay men don't hate you for loving women.
If you believe in God, you should not judge
others.
Love your son if he is gay.
If you are a victim of ignorance, read about and
speak to gay people.
Gay people struggle against ignorance, not
against God.
You have your beliefs and I have mine.
Let us spread love.

CHAPTER 5

Orgy in the Asylum Seekers' Building

Tea Time, Part 1

Every day at 5 pm, my flatmates would gather on the kitchen balcony to drink tea and watch the blonde woman who walked past the building every day at that time. She was middle-aged, tall, and she had a round face and tied her hair in a ponytail. She would often wear a yellow raincoat and purple wellies when she came prancing over the green space that surrounded the building in Åseda. She was never alone; we only ever saw this woman accompanied by a brown Labrador. One of my housemates would usually say, "I wish I was that big dog she's always with!"

Sometimes the dog gave us a comedy routine, especially when he cocked his back leg and showed off his droopy testicles and huge penis. The sight of it was enough to inspire several dirty jokes, but it made us laugh when the dog squatted and made a mess. Then the men would call to each other so the woman couldn't help noticing them as she gathered up the waste in a blue plastic bag and hung it on the dog's chain. This was their favourite part of the scene, and they couldn't help breaking out into respectful applause.

One unexpectedly crisp and sunny day in late September, my flatmates and I were on the balcony enjoying some fresh air, as the whole flat was filled with the smell of fried fish. That balcony was our greatest luxury owing to the view; as Wadih Al-Safi sang, our gaze fell upon forests "as far as the eye can see, and still the eye yearns for more." It was like a market for cheap, second-hand goods, where you could find everything the previous refugees had left behind: a dusty and wrinkled black leather jacket stuffed in the corner, an assortment of broken chairs of varying designs and sizes, an overturned, burned cooking pot. The broken mirror fragment resting on top of it reflected my loneliness and frustration. I was still waiting for my asylum claim to be dealt with by the Immigration Bureau. My roommate who arrived two weeks after me was lucky; he had been granted a residency permit and now rented a flat in the sub-urbs of Gothenburg. I was worried a new man would come and share my room after I had grown used to being alone.

I put on my red hoodie and pulled the hood up over my head so it barely showed my face, and leaned on the balcony railing while the woman walked past with her dog. Her stubborn dog forced her to stop precisely in front of our balcony. He started sniffing the damp grass. Abu Adnan, one of my flatmates, joined us in the kitchen. He had wrapped a large blue towel loosely around his waist, but the top of his pubic hair was showing. His hairy chest was bare, and I found his dark nipples incredibly attractive. He was carrying a glass cup brimming with hot tea. I scrutinised his body through half-covered eyes—I could even see the clear droplets on his chest hair. My mind drifted to the men I had slept with at the hammams in Damascus; they too used to drink tea after a long, leisurely bath. I longed to touch his damp chest.

"Are you crazy?"

It was Abu Muhammad who'd yelled. I took off my hood to work out whether he was speaking to me.

"Go and dry yourself or put on some pyjamas. It's too cold for that here."

Abu Muhammad, who also shared our flat, continued yelling at Abu Adnan. His loud voice drew the woman's attention. She gave us a broad, hopeful smile. I froze and noticed everyone on the balcony doing the same. Nobody knew how to react. The woman waved at us while the dog dragged her other hand by the chain, trying to run away.

"Salaam Aleikum!"

Nizar burst in, ash all over his beard and moustache from the cigarette dancing between his lips. He snatched the cigarette from his lips and pressed a kiss on each of our cheeks. After the cool breeze, his lips were warm on my face. I often considered Nizar the sexiest man in the building. He was a young father from Rif Dimashq and he was living in an apartment with his wife (who never said hello to anyone) and his daughter. I could never remember his wife's face but I clearly recalled the pure white hijab wound elegantly around her head, and the silver pin she used to fix it in place. Nizar was different from the other men in the refugees' building. He was the only man who preferred to be called by his first name; the others had nicknames that began with "Abu," meaning "father." Abu Muhammad, Abu Haydar, Abu George, and so on. Some of them weren't even fathers.

"You missed the woman and the dog with the huge dick. She cleaned up its shit," Abu Adnan welcomed Nizar as he dried off his chest with a small towel. As for me, I couldn't stop myself preparing a cup of tea for Nizar. Serving him gave me a kind of pleasure.

"They're nice people here," Nizar offered his sweeping opinion of the Swedish with a smile in his eyes. I placed the hot cup in his hand and sat next to him.

"They're even nice to dogs ... Perhaps that woman loves her dog more than her husband," said Abu Muhammad.

Nizar said, "Teresa. She's called Teresa. I heard the supermarket cashier call her that. She's also single!"

Nizar seemed confident in his information.

"That's why she has a dog," said Abu Maher before he exploded in a coughing fit that forced his head between his thighs. Abu Maher was a heavy smoker and sixty-four years old. He had lived in this building before I arrived, and two years before the rest of the younger men. His first asylum request had been refused because he claimed he came from the Eastern part of Syria, but really he was from Iraq. Abu Maher ... I could easily put myself in his shoes. We were all mixed together like the waters of the Euphrates, without much difference in features or social classes, and only a negligible difference in accent. When his appeal came before the Immigration Bureau, he confessed to being an Iraqi citizen. He was now waiting for the outcome of his appeal. Having arrived in Åseda before the rest of us, Abu Maher considered himself an expert on Sweden and the Swedes. He would tell us stories and make generalisations whose source, and point, were unclear. He explained Teresa's relationship with her dog as follows:

"Teresa has this dog for sexual enjoyment. Here in Sweden, women prefer sex with dogs over men."

Everyone burst out laughing, me included. At first I thought it was a joke until Abu Adnan said, "Do you think Abu Maher is joking? I always watch animal pornos where a hot woman falls onto a sofa and strikes some sexy poses and raises her legs so the dog can lick her cunt."

We all laughed again, even louder this time. The conversation turned to sex and how easy it is in a place like this. I noticed that Abu Adnan's nipples were becoming hard. He put the small towel he had used to dry his chest over his lap to cover his erection.

"I'd be lucky to be Teresa's dog and lick her pussy," said Abu Maher in a thick Iraqi accent.

"It's a tragedy that Teresa uses a dog when I'm right here," Nizar said in response.

As he said this, he stretched out an arm to indicate the length of his penis. Abu Adnan tugged his pubic hair and said Teresa was welcome to run wild in his forests—and her dog could come too. The atmosphere became increasingly charged, each provocative word dripping from their lips onto a pore of my skin. I pulled my hoodie off. The room became thick with their breathing and emotions. Their tongues licked their lips as they spoke about Teresa and imagined her there, in the room. I could read their body language and see the lust in their eyes. My eyes ran over the most sensitive parts of their bodies; I wanted them to strip off and finish what they had started in me. I wished I could be

Teresa and give my body to all these sexually re-pressed men to do what they wanted with. I hurried to the bathroom before I came in my trousers.

In the Bathroom

Nizar was waiting for me on tiptoe, naked beneath the hot shower. The steam couldn't block out the view, and I could make out every detail of his attractive face and his long, dark beard. He stared at my face with lust-filled eyes and, with his tongue running over his lips, he invited me closer. It was the first time I had seen him naked. His body seemed hard and the muscles of his broad shoulders stood out in relief. His arm bore an Arabic tattoo common among prisoners: *Ridaki ya Ummi*, "Bless you, Mum." There was hair over the upper part of his chest like an upturned pyramid that narrowed at the bottom, becoming a soft line that divided his flat stomach in two before it reached his pubic hair. His athletic, hairy arms moved steadily up and down as he stroked his huge penis.

I took off the rest of my clothes and tossed them onto the wet floor, then knelt down in front of Nizar and squeezed his thighs with my hands. I took a deep breath and inhaled the scent of laurel soap on his skin; it took me back to the hammams of Damascus. He leaned over me and his lips brushed the tip of my ear as he sweetly whispered, "Habibi."

Nizar brushed his fingers over my beard and al-lowed Abu Adnan to join us. Abu Adnan gently massaged my scalp with his large hands and rubbed his erection on my back. I was in the middle, kneeling between Abu Adnan and Nizar, and both of them started pressing against my body with the full weight of theirs. I felt under siege but I enjoyed what they were doing.

Abu Adnan was standing behind me, pushing me forward until my face met Nizar's penis. Abu Adnan's thick penis was moving against the back of my neck. The tip of Nizar's large penis met my cheek, a sign to me to touch it and give him even greater pleasure.

Nizar began to devour Abu Adnan's lips, their faces stuck together to become one. I let my hands discover the rest of Nizar's velvet-soft body; every pore was thirsting for love. Abu Adnan put his hands under my armpits and pulled me up a little, then pushed the back of my neck until I swallowed Nizar's cock. The hot water from the shower was crashing onto my back and the spray was going everywhere. Nizar planted his hands on my neck and pushed himself further down my throat, while Abu Adnan started lathering my ass with soap, using his thickset fingers to seek out a haven for his penis. When my body relaxed and I pressed myself against Abu Adnan, he seized his chance and with all his pent-up frustration thrust his cock between my buttocks. I was in heaven, watching Nizar moan in ecstasy, biting his lips and rolling his eyes upwards. I tried to indicate that Nizar should take Abu Adnan's place behind me, but instead he only pushed deeper into my mouth.

"Nija. Fuck him," cried Abu Maher hoarsely. He was standing at the bathroom door like a guard, watching us. He had uncovered his flabby chest covered in wiry grey hair. A towel was wrapped securely around his waist and his half-erect penis was tangled in the opening. He was like a randy old dog searching for some relief. He was horny but his flaccid penis precluded him from joining in.

"Fuck him, please fuck him!"

Abu Maher begged Nizar to fuck me—but Nizar didn't want to. Instead Nizar used one hand to squeeze my face, and the other to push his rigid penis deeper into my throat. The moment was close, and I was elated to humbly surrender my body to Nizar, to take everything he shot inside me.

I sat on the bathroom floor where water and soap mingled with my semen and gushed towards the drain. I rested my head against the cold porcelain tiles of the wall and wondered what the outcome would be if that scene had been real.

"Furat! Hurry up. Your new roommate has arrived," Abu Adnan yelled from behind the bathroom door.

Roommate

Sunlight filled my room. When I entered, I saw the silhouette of a short, skinny man in a baseball cap standing in the middle of the room, unpacking the same blue bag the immigration official had given me.

"Ahlan wa sahlan," I welcomed him, and I introduced myself. He returned the greeting and told me his name was Nidal. Next to him, there was a mud-encrusted backpack. He turned round and walked towards me, saying "Thank you" in a hesitant voice, accompanied by a gust of foul breath. When he smiled, I noticed his front teeth were missing. It was hard to guess his age from a brief glance at his exhausted, sunken eyes, wasted features, and light stubble. I asked him if he needed any help.

"That's all I've got," he said, pointing at the bed where he had put a tattered leather wallet, an orange toothbrush, a few coins, and a black plastic bag wrapped tightly shut with Sellotape.

His white shirt had an English phrase printed on it—*I Love Berlin*—which indicated his previous stopping point. I invited him to have dinner with me but he wanted to shower first. He took a towel and a bottle of shampoo from the blue bag. He asked if it was safe to leave his things on the bed while he was in the bathroom. I asked him to wait a moment and took a pair of briefs out of my drawer and handed them to him.

"They're clean," I said, and he took them with a grateful smile. He left me in the room with his things without a question, or even any apparent curiosity about his surroundings. He wasn't my type at all. That was a source of relief for me, seeing as I was sharing a room with him. If he had possessed Abu Adnan's allure, or Nizar's beauty, I would not have wanted to hazard a guess at how things might have transpired. I lay on my bed and closed my eyes, trying to find some sort of peace.

That night, I was woken from a deep sleep by the sound of Nidal snoring. Like many of the others, I found it hard to sleep in the refugees' building. I covered my head with the blanket, turned on my side, and put my hands over my ears, but when his snorts turned to moans and sobs, I was horrified.

Three days later I ran into Nidal in the kitchen while he was making some tea. By that point his beard had grown thicker.

"Did you sleep well last night?" he asked as he picked up the steaming mug in one hand and a rolled-up cigarette in the other, before heading to the balcony. He had spent the first twenty hours in bed. The second day, it was about eighteen hours. He was evidently a night owl.

I joined him on the balcony.

"Yes, I did," I said. Nidal crossed his arms over his chest.

"Are you cold?" I asked.

He didn't reply, but he gave me a searching look, then smiled.

In the few words Nidal had spoken to me, his accent indicated he was from the Yarmouk neighbourhood in Damascus. Nidal wasn't into speaking, and he seemed to prefer his own company. Since his arrival I had only seen him asleep or standing in the kitchen making black tea with vast quantities of sugar, and always smoking, or rolling cigarettes at the table. I never saw him cooking, not even making a sandwich. On the rare occasions he left the apartment, he took his backpack with him. He was obsessed with checking our apartment's mailbox.

He didn't seem to feel at all relaxed at having reached his final destination in Sweden, unlike the rest of the men who breathed a sigh of relief whenever they discussed the end of their journeys. This marked difference in him roused my curiosity: Was his a mysterious story or had he merely lost his family? Was he gay and so avoided associating with others? For me, he was a riddle that needed to be solved. One way or another he reminded me of myself when I first arrived. He kept himself separate from his surroundings and from others.

The sound of his thumb rasping insistently against his lighter brought me back to the present moment.

"Do you have a better lighter?" Nidal asked me.

"No, but I'm sure Abu Maher has lots," I said.

"No, no, no!" he replied.

When he wanted to leave the balcony, I guessed he was going to buy one. I got up and added, "Well, I also need to do some shopping in the ICA. Shall we go together?"

Parasomnia

Nidal flung the door open and strode over to my bed, panting. I was still lying there, having just woken up.

"You've had a letter from the Immigration Bureau. Maybe it's a decision about your residency."

He tossed a white envelope on my lap. I was still half-asleep. I got up, leaning my back against the wall. I put the pillow in my lap and the letter on top of the pillow.

"You're right. It's the Immigration Bureau."

I opened the envelope with a trembling hand. The letter was in Swedish, which I didn't know a word of. I picked up my phone—it was 10:24 on Tuesday morning, on the last day of September 2014—and I took a photo for Google Translate. I crumpled up the letter and threw it to one side.

"Ah ... It's a refusal."

"What?" cried Nidal.

"Don't worry, it's not the asylum request. It's just

for some winter clothes. The immigration official gave me some papers to request an allowance for winter clothes seeing as I arrived in summer. Every time she saw me, she reminded me about handing in the request, and now they've refused it. I can't see why."

I felt resentful and sad. Nidal sat on the edge of my bed and patted my shoulder.

"I might be deported soon. Even sooner than you imagine," said Nidal, and I could see tears in his eyes.

"I think we both need a cup of tea, ya sadiqi," I said. I got up and went to the kitchen and asked him to stay in the room.

The police had seized Nidal in Bulgaria, along with hundreds of other refugees. They were transferred to a holding centre somewhere in the countryside, a former Russian military base. When Nidal refused to give his fingerprints voluntarily, the police forced him to do so with their clubs. Nidal and a group of men devised a plan and escaped from the base, which was more like a prison both in appearance and the way it treated its inmates. After an arduous journey on foot and stowing away on trains, Nidal reached Malmö and put in his request for asylum. He was warned by the Immigration Bureau that his request might be refused. It seemed as though he wouldn't be here much longer.

Unexpectedly, both Abu Adnan and Abu Maher came into my room holding cigarettes and filling the air with smoke. They said, "We're taking the bus to Växjö to spend the night with some friends."

They asked me if I needed anything from the Arabic shop there while I sipped tea from Nidal's cup. I offered Abu Adnan and Abu Maher tea, but they were in a hurry to catch the bus.

"See you all tomorrow," they called as they left.

It was a mild, sunny day. Nidal and I did some shopping after we finished our tea. He had told me before that he had decided to be vegetarian in Europe as it was the easiest way of avoiding the dilemma of buying halal or non-halal meat. All he bought was cheese, cucumber, tomatoes, and flour. I paused at the Systembolaget and bought a bottle of red wine. I expected him to comment, or at least ask me about the alcohol, but he didn't. We went for a walk in the forest afterwards but, as usual, he didn't talk much. I, on the other hand, began to tell him my story in the forest; how I fell in love with it in the summer, how, as much as it dazzled me now, in its golden, autumnal garb it reminded me of my own loneliness. I took him to my favourite spot, deep within the forest—a huge boulder hidden by oak trees and surrounded by narrow streams. I told him it reminded me of the hot stones in the floors of the hammams in Damascus, where men would rest their backs. I was taken aback when he said the boulder reminded him of a grave.

On our way back to the building he told me he wanted to escape to Germany, and he was uncomfortable being in Sweden.

That evening we cooked and ate dinner together after I helped him bake Syrian bread, the first time I had made it in my life. There was comfort in the dough, and the smell of fresh bread that wafted through the kitchen made me feel at home.

We sat together at the kitchen table. I couldn't make out Nidal's face properly because of the steam coming from the oven behind him, the smoke from his cigarette, and the vapour from the hot tea in front of him. He asked me why I was so chatty and excited that day—I had sung while I was baking, and I even cleaned my room and the bathrooms without grumbling.

"I am more myself when the others go out."

"What do you do to feel like you when there's no one else around?"

"I dance. I move freely."

"Smoke?"

Nidal flicked an unlit cigarette in my direction; I didn't catch it in time so it fell on the floor. I picked it up and put it between my lips.

"This will be my first cigarette in Sweden."

"Did you stop smoking in Sweden?"

"No! I've never smoked. Even though when I was growing up, my brothers were heavy smokers."

He glanced at the ashtray in front of him, full of cigarette butts and ash. I found myself saying, "By the way, you remind me of my oldest brother. His wife is always complaining about that—the over-flowing ashtray."

Nidal remained silent while I began to talk about my family. I tried to draw him into conversation by asking him questions, but I failed. He began smoking even faster and wanted to fill his glass with more tea. He seemed surprised to find the teapot empty. He even opened the lid as if he was hoping to find a drop still in there.

"But you drink alcohol, don't you?" he asked. I didn't answer. I went to our room and came back with the bottle of wine I had bought earlier that day.

"Spanish red wine—Rioja."

I filled two glasses and offered him one. I raised the still-unlit cigarette between my forefinger and middle finger.

"Cheers!"

He automatically thanked me as he tried to light a cigarette.

Nidal had never drunk before but he wanted to try it because he had always heard that alcohol helped people forget their troubles. So far he had smoked half a carton of cigarettes while I left mine unlit, just flipping it over and over in my fingers. I refilled my glass while his was still as it was.

"Just the smell of wine is making me drunk, so what will happen if I drink it?" said Nidal when I suggested he take a sip.

"What was your journey like?" I asked.

I only wanted to make him more relaxed, to make him join in. I continued with my questions.

"Who was the best smuggler and who was the worst?"

"Is there a safer route than the death boats?"

"Which was the easiest border to cross?"

"One of my brothers is still stuck in Greece," I said. I kept talking about my brother's journey between Turkey and Greece, how he had refused to get on a boat because he couldn't swim and had a phobia of water, so he was forced to cross Greece's land border, which cost him double. He hid in the luggage compartment of a bus and afterwards he had to stay in a hospital in Athens for twenty-four hours to keep his breathing under observation.

My brother worried constantly about what would happen to his two-year-old daughter if something happened to him. I began to describe my niece to Nidal. I imitated how she would crinkle her face and stick out her bottom lip when she was angry, the way she waved her chubby little arms to explain something or justify her actions. I stood up so I could do a proper impersonation of her, and he could see my whole body. I imitated my niece dancing to Syrian music until I was no longer aware of what I was doing or where I was.

"My daughter is about the same age as your niece," Nidal said.

His face broke into a smile as he stood up next to me and started to talk about his daughter. He described her delicate hands, how she would put a pink plastic ring on her little finger. He was moving his hands, showing me how he would lift her up in the air when they were playing. He closed his eyes and talked about her as if he was reciting a poem written on the backs of his eyelids.

Her fingers are like pearls.

She loves applause and songs.

She grabs my fingers and laughs.

Her hair is in braids, the colour of blonde dates.

She laughs a lot and she cries a lot.

His words took my breath away. He spoke with a yearning that made me fear he had lost her along the journey, but these imagined fears disappeared when he said, "She is in Damascus with her mother, awaiting our reunion."

At this, I raised my glass joyfully and drank a gulp of wine. He raised his glass to me and smiled.

In 2013 I fled the siege of Yarmouk with my wife, my newborn daughter, and my younger brother, and together we went to Egypt. We settled in Alexandria where my brother and I found work as painters and construction workers. It was dirty and dangerous work. We didn't have any insurance. What choice did we have? If we didn't do that, all our savings for the journey to Europe would have been used up. You know what they say about trouble—it never rains but it pours. My wife got really sick and work dried up, we couldn't find anything. I couldn't afford my wife's treatment. We lost hope ... After a few hard months we decided to go to Europe by boat from Alexandria. That was in the summer of 2014. After two weeks of waiting, a smuggler called and told us not to bring any luggage apart from our documents. The address he gave us was in the middle of nowhere outside Alexandria. But there was no alternative. We went there and met another family of Palestinian Syrians, a couple with two children. The smuggler arrived in a small truck after dark. We had been there for a long time and were hungry and thirsty. My daughter was so tired and limp I had to carry her in my arms while my wife rested—she was sick and dizzy.

The smuggler had a strong Alexandrian accent. He did not seem very friendly. He told us to get into the truck. There were three young guys on board. We got in and it stank of cow dung. Another smuggler who had been sitting next to the driver got down and ordered us to turn off our phones and put them in the tote bag he was holding. In one corner of the truck there was a plastic bottle of water and a pile of sandwiches. My wife struggled to get in.

The truck set off at midday and only stopped when night fell. We were all exhausted, especially my wife, who was so weak she was like a corpse by that point. But we were determined to finish what we had started. The sound and smell of the sea revived me.

Suddenly out of the darkness, two men shouted: "Yalla yalla, bring them over here."

We were driven to a tiny wooden boat that already held several men. We were supposed to jump from this into a larger dinghy somewhere in the middle of the sea.

When we had sailed to the meeting point, a shouting match broke out between the smuggler in our boat and the smuggler in the dinghy opposite—they were fighting over the number of passengers they had to carry. There were more than fifty passengers in the dinghy, and it already looked on the verge of sinking. The tone of the fight escalated until there was a death threat. Our journey was cancelled. Our boat turned around and the smuggler told us we were on our way back to the place we had just left. I was so exhausted I didn't know what was happening.

Then things got worse—a gunshot rang out, the echo came from every direction. An angry voice yelled through a loudspeaker, "Do not return fire. We are the coastguard. We are the police."

The smuggler threw himself overboard. I stayed in the boat with my wife, my daughter, and the other family. We stared at each other without saying a word.

We were dumped in a cell in the police station in Awal Al-Raml in Alexandria. We ended the night in jail. The room was like a rotten rathole. We could hardly breathe. My daughter had a fever and my wife's illness got worse—I thought I would lose her that night. We asked the guards for help but they refused to even listen to us. A week later—thank God—the Egyptian police set us free. They returned our passports without a stamp and let us go ... to Damascus.

Confession

Nidal, his family, and I returned by plane to Damascus. My brother's wife's health worsened to the point where she was too weak to speak. There was no other way—we spent all our money on her treatment, knowing all the while the medicine was doing her no good. We had to make a decision: either we left his wife and child in Damascus and made the journey to Europe ourselves, or we stayed in Syria.

We chose to go without them. My brother would reunite with his wife and child as soon as he gained his residency permit. This time we cooperated with Syrian-Palestinian smugglers. Rumour had it they were working for the Mukhabarat and facilitating the evacuation of the camps full of Palestinians.

In Damascus Airport we were just a group of Palestinian men heading to Qamishli in northeast Syria. When we went through security, and the official tried to find out the real reason we were heading for Qamishli, we said we had been invited to a

Kurdish wedding. After we got on the plane the shabiha came on board. They were carrying assault rifles. They forced everyone to hand over 10,000 Syrian liras without bothering to come up with any justification.

Before the shabiha left, a clean-shaven bald man turned and spat on us. "You bastards, you sons of whores. We know you're all going to Germany. The president knows every hair on your wives' pussies."

I gripped my brother's hand and couldn't work out which one was soaked, his hand or mine. We spent two nights in northern Syria until we were smuggled across the border with the same group of men we had travelled with on the plane. The whole group clung to each other. We spent over a month in Izmir.

We couldn't do anything but wait until the smugglers gave us an indication that the next stage of our journey had been arranged. This gave me time to think and helped me grasp what I and my brother and the others were going through. I started to see new things in my brother. He spoke all the time about his daughter, about his big dreams for providing a safe life for her. He told me he could face every danger to ensure his daughter would grow up in a country where she would have an easier life. His daughter was at the heart of everything he said.

Once, when we were out buying life jackets, my brother asked the shopkeeper if he had one for a two-year-old child. I prayed to God: "Lord, if the boat capsizes and one of us has to die ... let it be me. Please, choose me, Lord, if you want to take one of us." But neither God nor Nidal heard my prayer. Nidal drowned, and it was me who was left alive.

What was he saying? Who was Nidal and who was the brother? Who was this man sitting in front me? Was I drunk or sober? I couldn't understand. I wanted to refill my wineglass but the bottle was empty. I bumped into Nidal's glass and raised it to my mouth before I realised it too was empty. With that, I dragged my heavy body to my room, shut the door, and collapsed on the bed. I buried my face in the pillow.

I could still hear voices coming from the kitchen. Heavy footsteps. A door closing, a drawer opening. Furtive movement. The main door of the apartment unlocking and opening. Footsteps approaching our room, stopping at the door. I sank my face deeper and deeper into the pillow. darkness within me. This inner darkness was as vast as the sea, illuminated by a shame that seemed to go on forever. The only barrier between the two darknesses was my eyelids.

In my oblivion I fell into a clear blue sea and rays of sunlight surrounded me. They deceived me and vanished whenever I tried to catch hold of them. I sank and sank until I fell into the lap of Abu Adnan, who was naked at the bottom of the sea. He held me tight, and I felt safe. He let me squirm in his lap like a fish until I was just a head between his thighs. I rested my cheek on his pubic hair, inhaled the scent of his musky sweat, tasted the salt on his skin. I buried my face between his thighs. My heart began to beat faster, and I squeezed against his body until a warm liquid spurted over my legs.

"Where's Nidal?"

A voice woke me.

I could hardly open my eyes. I found myself looking at Nidal's face, printed onto a sheet of A4 paper. Two police officers were standing by my bed holding his photo. They left without getting any answer from me. I got up off the bed and a sharp headache pulsed through my head. I walked to the bathroom to glance at my face and found the underwear I had given Nidal on my laundry basket. When I walked to the kitchen I found it was clean and tidy. The ashtray, tea pot, and glass cups were empty and sitting on the table. I guessed that Nidal and his backpack had left on the first bus out of Åseda at 5:45.

There was a noise outside the building. I went out onto the balcony and looked down. The same police officers were outside the building, speaking with Abu Adnan, Abu Muhammad, Abu Maher, and others, showing them a photo of Nidal. I leaned over and put my arms on the railing. The blonde woman Nizar had called Teresa was, as usual, strolling slowly and hopefully past with her dog, but this time no one from the building noticed her. All eyes were focused on Nidal's face in the hands of the police.

I leaned back and crossed my arms over my chest, just as Nidal used to do. I looked towards the horizon where the colourful autumn trees appeared, and I recited Kahlil Gibran's lines to myself:

There is no justice in the forest ... no, nor is there punishment

If the willow casts its shade over the soil

The cypress does not say this heresy against the Book

The justice of people is snow—the sun would see it melted.

Give me the ney and a song, for song is the justice of hearts

And the wail of the ney remains long after sins have been annihilated.

CHAPTER 6

Qur'ans

The Red Qur'an

When I was very young, I got to know the Qur'an in the shape of a huge, red book in the hands of my widowed mother. This Qur'an was her intimate friend and companion at every occasion following my father's death. When she had finished reading it, she would carefully replace it on its own special stand. This stand was an antique in itself, carved from walnut and inlaid with mother-of-pearl and copper. I used to spend hours standing in front of the red Qur'an, lost in contemplation. It was broader than my shoulders and larger than my school dictation notebook. I was in the habit of touching it furtively. I would sweep my small fingers over the reliefs like a blind man, feeling the long minarets with crescent moons at their summits, the Kaaba and ornate galleries of mosques embossed on the red leather in black and gold. The book was too heavy for me to lift and whenever I tried to turn the pages, I failed. But I would inhale the perfume that emanated from its pages, which smelled just like my mother's hands. Whenever I looked at the red Qur'an, I felt a light surrounding it. I believed it had descended to our house from heaven, until my mother told me it was a gift from her father, who had bought it for her when he performed the Hajj pilgrimage in the seventies.

As I grew older, the Qur'an looked smaller than it did before. I learned how to wash my face, hands, elbows and the back of my neck, even my feet, so I could touch it with my hands and turn its pages openly rather than in secret. At last I was able to open the red Qur'an. Its lines were dazzling to me, every page a work of art. It became my obsession. I didn't understand what was written in it but I met the challenge head-on and was resolved to recite it and learn it by heart. After finishing my homework, I would sit down in front of the stand and do my best to decipher it. Through the red Qur'an I learned the word *myth*, a new word and a difficult one for a child of my age, but I memorised it all the same. I liked the way it was written and practiced writing it out myself. I began to use it in my speech, sometimes appropriately, sometimes incorrectly, and my siblings would make fun of me. An intimate relationship sprang up between the red Qur'an and me. We became good friends, and it began to sleep in my bed next to me instead of my toys. My mother was pleased by this new friendship and told me it would keep the nightmares away.

The Yellow Qur'an

Like many who spent their childhood in the city of Deir Ezzor, the first piece of information I learned about my life was that I was born in Mesopotamia, where human civilisation began. My first school trip was to the kingdom of Mari, founded 2,900 years BCE.

The Euphrates divides my city into several banks, as the river branches off into two streams. The first, larger branch, where the island of Hawijat Kati lies, was the site of the famous suspension bridge. This bridge was built during the French occupation in the 1920s. A French architect designed it, and the townspeople built it. It ended up taking more than six years, and the lives of scores of workers. It was even said by some elderly inhabitants of Deir Ezzor that a few of the workers fell into the concrete moulds that held the bridge up while the cement was being poured in, and their bodies are still there now. It is considered the second suspension bridge in the world after the one in the south of France, and so the people of Deir Ezzor consider it a symbol of their city, as well as a source of joy and pride. Everyone in Deir Ezzor has memories of that bridge. There was barely a house in the city, ours included, that did not have photos of family members leaping from it into the river, or as the backdrop to a gathering of family or friends, or even a wedding photo—it used to be a custom in the city for a newlywed groom to take his bride for a walk over the bridge or along the riverbank.

Despite the wide river and the orchards lining its banks, my principal memory of Deir Ezzor is the dull colour of its dusty, dry soil. It tainted everything; the drab grey on the riverbanks could also be seen on the plains surrounding the city. The foxes, rabbits, gazelles, wolves, and hyenas were dust-coloured as well; even the birds were the same shade as the mountain that was a graveyard for the city's dead.

And the walls of the ancient houses were made of mud and stone, like a continuation of the soil.

The churches and mosques were all the same colour as well. The character of the city was Christian, originating from its name Deir—in Aramaic, the language of the Messiah, *deir* means "house of the farmer," referring to the monks' way of life. In Arabic, *deir* only refers to the place where monks and nuns live, those who spend the greater part of their time in worship and contemplation. Muslims and Christians divided the city. Many Armenians sought refuge in Deir Ezzor after the massacres perpetrated by the Ottoman Empire between 1914 and 1923 and they lived among the people of Deir Ezzor and began to work, often specialising in the repair of cars and watches. In 1990, I sat on my big brother's shoulders, resting my small legs on his chest and holding tight onto his hair, to watch the inauguration of the Church of Armenian Martyrs in the presence of the Catholicos of All Armenians from the Holy See of Cilicia. After that, Armenians from all over the country began visiting Deir Ezzor on the 24th of April every year to commemorate the victims of the genocide. The memory of the Armenian massacres didn't die in the memory of the people of Deir Ezzor; they considered it an integral part of the city's history.

In the mid-eighties, our father inherited a very large house with a garden like an orchard wrapped all around it, but he died of a heart attack within a year of moving there. Our neighbourhood was called Qusour. It, too, was dust-coloured despite having many parks. Even though it was only a kilometre from Joura—the poorest and most deprived area of Deir Ezzor—Qusour was considered the most prestigious neighbourhood in the city and by far the cleanest. It had wide streets lined with tall, orderly palm trees. Best of all, in the heart of the neighbourhood lay an enormous mosque, the largest and grandest in the city. It was famed for its up-to-date cooling system and, given that the climate of Deir Ezzor was usually hot, men from all over the city headed to our neighbourhood every Friday for prayers. The houses in Qusour, as the name suggests, were shaped like small palaces, their windows distinguished by their long wooden shades, and surrounded by gardens filled with tall poplar trees. Our neighbours were some of the city's wealthiest, drawn from traders and rich, cultured families. Later, doctors moved in, along with officials, such as the director of the central prison and the chief of police; because of this, the electricity company never cut off the power there. It was also the neighbourhood of choice for foreign consultants who worked in the oilfields surrounding the city. A Canadian petroleum engineer lived in the villa opposite our house. He had a black and white dog, beautiful and tame, who used to love escaping and napping in the shade of our garden's many trees.

One hot summer morning when I was nine I saw some boys roughly my age standing on the pavement outside the neighbourhood mosque. Most of them were wearing white, with caps of the same colour on their heads, and they were carrying white school bags. They were getting into a minibus that was white too. Everything was white. I spotted Nishwan, our neighbour's son, among them, and asked if he was going on Hajj. Giggling, he said, "No, we're students at the

Hafez Assad Institute for Memorising the Qur'an, here at the mosque. This is the day we go to the swimming pool." He got on the bus with his friends, their eyes filled with excitement. I raced home and as soon as my mother opened the door I said, "I want to join the Hafez Assad Institute for Memorising the Qur'an." My older brother's voice came from his room: "Our little brother wants to become the little sheikh." I didn't know what my brother meant until I grew up and read that Nietzsche's friends had called him "the little pastor" in his youth for his ability to recite the Gospels in an affecting voice.

The following day was my first at the institute. It was the first time I had ever been inside the mosque. I wasn't like the other boys—instead of a white thobe or a kufi cap, I was wearing denim dungarees and a colourful T-shirt. I sat next to the other boys on the floor where we made a ring in the middle of the mosque, waiting for the sheikh to arrive. I was dazzled by the mosque's whiteness, vast and beautiful, like a wedding hall. It felt like being in a cloud. Everything gleamed—the tall windows, the stained glass, the high ceiling, the dozens of crystal lanterns hanging from it in different shapes like stars. I was filled with awe when I saw the mosque's dome from the inside. A huge, glittering chandelier descended from it like the sun, the same shade of gold as my mother's bracelets, filled with small lights and countless pieces of delicate crystal. It was astonishing, but I was afraid it would fall on my head, so I quickly moved to a spot in front of the imam's mihrab where I was not directly beneath it. This mihrab was similar to the stand where the red Qur'an was kept in our house, the same kind of wood inlaid with mother-of-pearl, and I felt comforted as I looked at it. The floor was furnished with a Persian rug featuring a pattern of repeating columns that was soft to the touch and comfortable to sit on—it was a work of art. My mother had told me the mosque was a dowry for Najla, the breathtakingly beautiful daughter of our neighbour. A wealthy businessman from Baghdad had met Najla in the seventies when he was visiting Deir Ezzor with his family in search of a Syrian bride. His visit culminated in his marriage to Najla in exchange for an unbelievable dowry; one of its clauses was to build a huge mosque in our neighbourhood. I hadn't yet met Najla's children because of the rift between the presidents of Syria and Iraq at the end of the seventies. There had been a power struggle over who would rule if the two nations were unified and, immediately after this, relations between the two countries were severed and the citizens of each country could no longer freely cross the border. Hafez Assad's refusal to join Iraq in waging war on Iran further stoked the tension, which particularly affected the people of Deir Ezzor, as many of its families lived between Syria and Iraq.

Despite the soaring temperatures outside, the mosque was very cold because of the air conditioning. My shoulders were shivering, and I rubbed my feet together to keep warm. Before long the students were all present, and the circle was complete. A huge man with the appearance of a sheikh approached us carrying a tote bag. The student next to me whispered, "That is the sheikh." The sheikh handed me a yellow booklet with the title 'Umm. And so I got to know a new Qur'an. It was very slim and light compared to the red Qur'an at home, no more than twenty pages. It smelled like a new schoolbook. On the back cover in black Naskh script was the legend *Printed in Deir Ezzor.* The sheikh said, "Write out your full name and your home telephone number. This is the last part of the Qur'an, and we will begin the lesson here." I asked him why we were learning the Qur'an back to front. He was annoyed by this, fell silent and knitted his eyebrows. He stroked his fingers through his grey beard for a moment and when he spoke, he asked my name and my family name.

The sheikh seemed to be in his forties. His beard was the length of a fist, and he wore large glasses that did little to conceal his harsh features. While he was reciting the Qur'an I meditated on his appearance and imagined him in clothes other than his jalabiya and turban. I imagined him dressed like Father Christmas, or in the clothes of our Canadian neighbour who invariably wore khaki shorts, a white T-shirt with a company logo on it, and a red cap on his head. All my fantasies faded away when he asked me to recite Surah Al-Nas for him. The sheikh did not have much praise for my recital, even though I was certain my pronunciation was sound and I had observed all the tashkeel.

Once class was over I went straight home and opened the red Qur'an. The words there seemed much more beautiful. My mother listened as I recited the surah the sheikh had explained to us, and she said I recited it with great sensitivity and without any mistakes.

I endured six days of the sheikh's doltishness to get to the seventh: the day there was swimming after class. I got onto the minibus with the boys I had seen the week before. I sat next to Nishwan, our neighbour's son, a mischievous kid who liked to clown around and crack jokes. I didn't understand them but I laughed along with the others. Nishwan asked me, "What's the long thing that white stuff comes out of?" One of the other boys jumped in: "The pilgrims' bus." All the boys cackled and again I joined in although I didn't get the joke. Nishwan kept hurling questions at us, all involving something long and something else coming out of it. Once it was kids, another time it was liquid, and the boys kept shrieking with laughter. Suddenly they all shut up. The sheikh got on the bus and sat down next to the driver. The bus set off, and after about twenty minutes we arrived at the swimming pool.

I was the first one to take off my clothes. I raced to the pool in just my swim shorts but was terrified when the sheikh called me by my name and stopped me from going in the pool. He said that what I was wearing was against sharia and told me to put my clothes back on and sit next to him. After he had finished reciting the safety rules to the others, he turned to me and said, "You must cover up your awra next time." I didn't understand what he meant by "awra." He pointed to the other boys who were all wearing loose swimming trunks that covered their knees. He told me if I wanted to go swimming, I had to wear something like them. He told me he owned a shop that sold appropriate clothes. He wrote down the address on the first page of my booklet and told me to give the address to my mother, and she would know what to do. I spent the day sitting in the shade of a tree, covering my eyes so I wouldn't remember anything about the place. The boys finished swimming and we all piled back onto the bus. I pretended to sleep all the way home. I didn't want to speak to anyone. As soon as the bus halted in front of the mosque, I ran home.

I didn't tell my mother what had happened. I was afraid she would stop me from wearing my beloved blue swim shorts and buy me trunks that covered my knees instead. I was totally in love with the white sea waves printed on my shorts. Whenever I put them on, I felt like a sea captain, and I set sail in my daydreams and drifted away to choose a sea and a distant harbour. I had received these shorts for my eighth birthday; my uncle had bought them for me on a trip to Lattakia.

I put the booklet underneath my pillow so it wouldn't fall into the hands of my mother or one of my siblings, and I fell asleep.

The following day I went to the Qur'an study session at the usual time. The class was longer than usual but I sat patiently all the way to the end. As soon as the sheikh ordered us to leave I went to the bathroom with my bag and turned the tap on full as if I was going to perform wudu. Cautiously, I took the booklet out of my bag and opened it. On the top of the first page my full name and telephone number were written in my handwriting; next to them, in his handwriting, was the address of the sheikh's shop. In the middle of the page, Surah Al-Fatiha was printed in large, Ottoman-style script. I ripped out the page, folded it, put it quietly in my pocket, and left the bathrooms. The hall of the mosque had emptied completely.

I walked on tiptoe over the soft carpet, towards the

shelves in the corner that were reserved for copies of the Qur'an. I looked over my shoulder to make sure no one was looking. After checking the first page was still safely in my pocket, I stuck the booklet in between the copies of the Qur'an that had been frozen by the air-conditioning. I headed to the wooden mihrab, gazing at the beautiful pictures carved there. I was sad to think I would never see it again. I left the mosque.

My footsteps were sluggish and hesitant as I headed home. The page in my pocket pressed on me like a physical weight. I wasn't sure why I had kept it when I didn't want any trace of Sheikh Ustaz around me, but I couldn't throw it in the bin because the words of God were written on it. After a few hours spent contemplating the matter on the swing in the park opposite our house, I remembered how my grandmother used to burn the Islamic almanac at the end of the hijri year so the Qur'anic verses wouldn't fly away to unclean places or rubbish heaps. I headed to the cigarette kiosk to avoid the question from the neighbourhood grocer: "Why are you buying matches instead of an ice cream today?" I went inside the kiosk for the first time. The owner was a young guy, deep in conversation on his phone. He waved at me to wait. I stood contemplating the freezer full of ice cream in the middle of the kiosk. It had a poster stuck on it that showed a blonde girl wearing an orange dress with a vertical yellow line down the side. She was standing on a beach, arms raised, look- ing at me as if she knew me and was inviting me to join the group of half-naked young men surrounding her, their hands around her tiny waist. The girl be- witched me, and I began scrutinising her expression, reading her eyes. "You like her? You're too young for that," the shopkeeper's voice interrupted my musings. Then he said: "Her name's Madonna. They call her the Queen of Pop—and of Sex, too." He laughed out loud then said, "What kind of ice cream do you want?" I turned around to make sure no one was watching then replied in a low voice, "Matches—I want a box of matches."

I slunk back to the neighbourhood and went up to the roof before the sun set. I glanced over my shoulder to make sure no one was watching. With a trembling hand I rolled the paper up into a cigarette shape so the words were hidden. It was the first time in my life I had struck a match to destroy something.

The School Qur'an

The Qur'an can simply be pages in a schoolbook. This one was a religious book filled with Qur'anic verses, stuffed in my bag just like a reading book or a science textbook. In middle school, the book of Islamic Education focused on sex, since we were going through puberty. Because of the lack of religious schools in the city they tasked Mr. Mumtaz, who taught Arabic Language, with Islamic Education as well. Mr. Mumtaz was a neighbour of ours, notorious for his love of wine, verse, and women. His wife had forced him into a divorce because of his tendency to drink and his repeated infidelities. He was renowned for his thick, long hair that was always combed and daubed with oil. He left the top buttons of his shirt undone to show off his broad, brown-skinned chest covered with hair and the thick gold chain wound around his neck. He put a golden watch around his wrist; choked his fat finger with a large gold ring set with a wine-coloured gemstone; and set a misbaha of black agate dancing between his fingers. Tuesdays with Mr. Mumtaz were always memorable. He had to stay in our classroom for the first three hours of the day, for two consecutive lessons: first he taught us Arabic language and then he would turn into the religion teacher.

In the classroom, we "Assad cubs" were blueprints for young soldiers. We all wore a khaki school uniform and were packed side by side in the chairs in the grey classroom. As I was so short, I sat in the first chair in the front row, directly opposite the picture of Hafez Assad on the wall above the blackboard painted the colour of oil. That same picture of Hafez Assad was on my desk too, on the cover of the notebook in front of me. Mr. Mumtaz finished the Arabic lesson. He was infatuated with the poets of the Mahjar and the Pen League, and often recited some verses from Kahlil Gibran's poem "Al-Mawakib."

Did you bathe in perfume and dry yourself with light?
Did you drink the dawn like wine in cups of ether?
Give me the ney and sing, for song is the secret of eternity
And the wail of the ney remains after life is extinguished.

He never cared if the language lesson ran over at the expense of the time allotted for religion. One particular Tuesday he stole ten minutes of it. Then he closed the Arabic language textbook, put it in his bag, and asked us to get out our Islamic education books. Mr. Mumtaz was so huge he covered the face of Hafez Assad entirely if he sat on the edge of the table in front of me. When he spread his legs, the outlines of his testicles and limp penis were clearly visible through his cotton trousers. In that lesson, he didn't use any references or books to speak to us. He began to talk straight away as if he had written the book himself.

He spoke about the external changes that would happen to our bodies when we became men, about armpit hair, pubic hair, and hair on our legs. I felt as though he had taken all my clothes off and shown everyone the hair that had begun to sprout on my crotch and legs. He talked about *the secret habit* and said he was certain we were all doing it and it was haram. He spoke about men's fertile imaginations while engaged in this practice, picturing themselves undressing women and ravishing them. I interrupted him: "Do women do it too?" He replied, "Of course. When you grow up, you'll see."

He told us these imaginings were halal as long as the sex was only in our dreams. The voice of a student came from the back: "What happens during a wet dream?" The teacher said, "You horny dog." We all laughed. In response he gave us an elaborate description of the body of a naked woman: breasts and thighs and arse. Then he spoke about the sensation of fucking in a dream as though it were real. "You wake up and it's as though your cock is inside a warm cunt," he said dreamily. "And the woman is already naked, so you don't waste any time undressing her." Mr. Mumtaz talked about the fluids secreted by the vagina to facilitate penetration. He closed his eyes and waxed lyrical about pleasure, orgasm, fluids, and ejaculation. I turned around to make sure no one was watching me. And then I closely observed the various stages of Mr. Mumtaz's erection, how the head of his cock swelled and grew large, trapped between the fabric of his trousers and his thighs, just like the cocks I later saw in the drawings of Tom of Finland. I fixed my eyes on it; my gaze ripped the cloth. I was face to face with an erect penis for the first time. I remember it so well I even drew it on a page in my notebook while writing this paragraph.

The smell of semen filled the classroom. There were more than forty of us and I swear half of us started puberty during that lesson. The other half probably came in their underwear. Mr. Mumtaz asked me to open the window. A cool breeze blew over my face, Mr. Mumtaz, and the other students. Then Mr. Mumtaz asked me to close the window and sit back down in my seat; he changed the subject and began to talk about grave sins and fornication.

The most beautiful part of that age was the madness of adolescence. After school we used to go straight to Hawija, the island in the Euphrates. There was no bridge to Hawija and the only way of getting there was by rowboat, so we used to beg a rowboat owner to take us. If we couldn't find anyone, we would swim the 400 metres and arrive at Hawija exhausted. We would rest on the beach for a little while then start playing around. We would climb the trees together and pick apricots, greengages, and small apples the size of cherries that tasted like honey. The farmers' dogs would bark at us and sometimes they chased us like thieves. At last, when we were tired, we would all sit together in the shade of a tree to talk about our youth, our dreams, and our country. My friends used to talk about girls' schools, where they would lurk outside the gates for hours. They were risking the hair on their heads, as the saying goes. Although it wasn't just a saying—the police could seize young men standing at the school gates and shave their head to the scalp in front of the girls, just like shearers did to their sheep on the pavement in the animal market. As for me, rainbow colours were already lighting up my heart. While they found the girls' school the most exciting place to be, for me it was the mosque, especially during Friday prayers, when hundreds of bearded men arrived in throngs, wearing sparkling white thobes that showed off their hairy legs and bare feet with hair covering their thick toes all the way to their clean, carefully pared nails. Those days, I was assiduous about attending the mosque as if it was a party. I would perform my wudu, and I repeated verses of poetry the Arabic language teacher used to recite.

Have you bathed in perfume and dried yourself in light, did you drink the dawn like wine in cups of ether?

I would slip out of the house and head to the mosque every Friday, supposedly for prayers. But in truth I spent the time in the café opposite, stealing glances at the men as they left; in their white thobes, they appeared like a thick, white stream gushing down the stairs. I watched them illuminated by sunlight, gathering around the hawkers' carts, selecting fruit and vegetables by pressing them with their thick fingers, chatting and laughing so their white, even teeth showed through their beards and moustaches. Some still had a toothpick in their mouths as they chatted with the sellers. The best moments were when someone mounted a bike and raised his white thobe so his legs and thighs were revealed. I only left the café when the scene was completely emptied of white.

The Coloured Qur'ans

As the years passed I got to know other Qur'ans: the blue pocket-sized Qur'an in my aunt's handbag to protect her from the evil eye; the large black Qur'an on the shelf in my lawyer uncle's office to give him credibility; the brown Qur'an belonging to our neighbour Um Hamada, which she took with her every time she left the house so she could put her right hand on it and swear she was innocent—she had never hit her son Hamada, and her divorced husband had unjustly taken her son away with his lies.

I started attending the University of Aleppo. There wasn't any religion class and it was rare that I looked at a Qur'an in those days, but when I visited my mother's house, I would see the red Qur'an in her hands, and the image still retained its sanctity for me. However, just like the red Qur'an itself, my relationship with it became distinctly touristic. I saw its wooden stand only as an artefact.

The Qur'an and the Revolution

In Deir Ezzor, the 2011 uprising against the regime of Assad's son began in Joura, the impoverished neighbourhood nearby, and it didn't take long to reach ours. The Assadist army and its shabiha delivered a devastating blow to the city. Their tanks destroyed our neighbourhood mosque, bombing it during Friday prayer. It was said that Sheikh Ustaz's head was sent flying the moment he claimed victory for Bashar Assad. Najla, our neighbour's daughter who had fled to Deir Ezzor with her millionaire husband after the Americans struck Baghdad, escaped once again, this time to Turkey and on foot. Our neighbour Um Hamada was avenged when a knife was rammed into her unjust ex-husband's heart. Our middle school became an arsenal for the Free Army. The Church for the Armenian Martyrs was razed to the ground. The suspension bridge was destroyed and swallowed by the river, along with all who were on it. Hawija was besieged by unknown forces and its gardens and meadows set alight. The shabiha executed the owner of the cigarette kiosk, tied his legs together with a thick rope, hung him from the back of a car, and dragged him around the neighbourhood for everyone to see, all because he had taken a protestor to hospital after they were shot. A sniper killed our neighbour Abu Nishwan on his way home from praying at the mosque. Another rooftop sniper shot his son Nishwan in the head as he was pulling his father's corpse to shelter. The same sniper shot my uncle Mahmoud in the head as he knocked on our door; he had come to see my mother, whose body was being devoured by cancer. My aunt Salma died that same night after seeing a video of my uncle's body on TV while she was watching the news. Exactly a week later, my mother died.

I opened the smooth gold lock of a pearl necklace hanging around my mother's neck. My father had brought it for her from Bahrain as a gift for her fortieth birthday and she always said she would only take it off when she died. I put it in her wooden box alongside her golden bracelets and jewellery. I took the red Qur'an from its stand and recited Surah Yasin over her head. My mother had died, and my secret had died with her. I had told her I was gay five years before her death, during her afternoon coffee, and she received the news like it was a dry biscuit that required dipping in her coffee. "If it makes you happy, enjoy it and hold onto it," she said with a last sip of coffee. But the next day she came to me and suggested I marry the daughter of her friend, a twenty-year-old girl who had never finished her education. She was the first and last woman I really knew in my life; she played the role of father and mother to me and my siblings, and she was my reference point for all women.

The road to the family graveyard was closed—it was on the other side of the city's front line. Before darkness fell my three siblings picked up my mother's emaciated corpse and went to the neighbourhood park to bury her. I was at the back of the funeral procession. I turned around to make sure no one was watching me; I didn't want anyone to see that I was afraid of the burial rites. The others dug a grave and placed my mother's body inside. They covered her with the same soil that used to cling beneath my fingernails after playing in the park; she always had to scrub it off when she bathed me. My mother rested in the park next to her brother. Death had betrayed her again. First, it took her husband from her when she was still in her youth, and today it deprived her of lying beside him. I went closer to her to recite Surah Al-Fatiha with my siblings, but before I could raise my hands to start praying a gunshot rang out and almost deafened me.

Instantly we dropped to the ground. I fell right on top of my mother's grave and the soil went into my mouth; her grave got stuck between my teeth. I breathed in her perfume through the earth. The firing stopped, and the sound of women and children screaming took its place. "They've killed someone," my brother whispered. We could hear windows being smashed, iron gates being pushed open with guns. Some shabiha started shouting: "Come on, you son of a bitch. Come and face us, you cunts. Fuck you and your sister's cunt."

After this incident, it was two months before we were able to go back to the family home. There was blood everywhere. Blood on the wall. Blood on the table. Blood on the shattered glass. Blood on the shrivelled plants. Blood on the television. Blood on the broken plates. Our furniture was smashed up and stained with blood. The contents of the shelves had ended up on the floor. They had even pulled down the curtains, torn them up, and thrown them on the living room floor. I lifted the fabric from the floor and found the red Qur'an underneath, its cover open like a woman screaming in distress. Its pages were torn and scattered, and the outline of a military boot was printed on them. I threw the curtains to one side and hugged the Qur'an. *They killed you.*

I gathered up all the pages I could find that weren't

bloodstained and placed them inside the red cover. I looked for the stand, but I couldn't find it anywhere. They had looted the rare antique and torn up the Qur'an before tossing it aside. My brother's voice came from my mother's room. "They stole a dead woman's jewellery. Her pearl necklace is gone."

The Qur'an in Danger

The Queen of Pop filled the stage of the BRIT Awards with her black cloak, standing firm and singing "Living For Love." Masked dancers with lithe bodies and bare chests leapt around her like bulls as she sang, "You empowered me, you made me strong, built me up and I can do no wrong."

The dancers pulled off her cloak like they were pulling the rug from beneath her feet. Madonna stumbled and fell, and the matador costume she was wearing underneath the cape was revealed. The dancers froze, waiting for her to make her own decision. Madonna got up and carried on singing. I didn't find the clip funny—I admired the way she took charge and simply began again. I watched the clip over and over.

Those short clips were like medicine for me as I lay in bed in the asylboende.

"Watch the moment Madonna falls onstage" was the most-watched video on Facebook at the time. The next video showed a nine-year-old child from Deir Ezzor, now a refugee in Beirut. He was sitting in a warehouse full of mineral water, singing a mournful mawwal from the Euphrates region. As they say in my dialect, "it nourished my heart" to hear his sweet voice singing of loss, but I couldn't bear to watch the video all the way through and skipped to the next.

The red Qur'an filled my phone screen. It was my mother's Qur'an in every detail: the long minarets with crescent moons on top, the drawing of the Kaaba, the galleries of mosques, all embossed in black and gold. At the edge of the screen was the title: *Execution of a young man from Deir Ezzor*. A man's voice boomed, "In the Name of God, the Merciful, the Compassionate." I became deaf after that phrase.

Zoom out.

The red Qur'an was being held by a huge man wearing a loose black robe and a black covering over his face. He was standing in front of a beige curtain. In his other hand he raised a silver sword that gleamed like it was fresh from the ironmonger's.

Zoom out.

A teenage boy appeared next to the man swathed in black. This boy was on his knees, looking at the ground. His hair was brown and curly, like a large bouquet tied with a black ribbon. It reminded me of our neighbour Hamada's hair—we used to call him Hamada the Sheep. *Hamada, Hamada, Hamada*, a voice inside me started screaming. I looked closer. That was Hamada's hair. I looked at his surroundings. *Our curtains, our curtains, our curtains in my mother's living room*. My tongue was paralysed but my heart was howling inside my ribs. *Our house, our house, our house*. The masked man brought down the sword and cut off Hamada's head. His beautiful bouquet of hair fell to the ground.

With trembling fingers, I turned off my phone and hid it under my pillow. I sat on top of it. I put my head under the pillow. I put my hand under the pillow. I annihilated my tear-stained face in the pillow. The pillow the pillow the pillow. I picked up the phone again. I didn't dare switch it on. I put it in my drawer next to my underwear. I turned around to make sure no one was watching me. I pulled out my bag from under the bed, lifted it up, put it on my thighs, and opened it. The cover of the red Qur'an appeared. I shut the bag. I opened it. I shut it. I opened it. I shut it. I opened the drawer, took my phone, and turned it on. I went onto Facebook and realised all my friends had shared the video. *Execution of a young man from Deir Ezzor*. The man holding the red Qur'an was murdering a young man from Deir Ezzor. Watch Hamada be murdered before deleting. Before deleting before deleting before deleting watch before deleting. Watch Hamada's murder.

That was Hamada, those were our curtains, that was our house, that was my mother's Qur'an ... They killed Hamada in our house. Our house had been turned into an execution chamber.

I felt as if I was being lifted up above my bed. My feet couldn't find the ground. I jumped like someone throwing themselves into the abyss. I lay my head on the ground. I crawled to the door. I didn't dare open it. I peered through the crack at the bottom and found only cat's claws. I rushed to the window to throw myself out, but I didn't dare open it. I didn't want anyone to come in, not even the wind. I took my towel from the drawer and blocked the crack at the bottom of the door. I hid under the bed. I lay on the ground and rested my head on my bag. I hugged the bag. I rested my head on it. I hugged the bag. I rested my head on it.

The red Qur'an escaped the bag and flew around the room like a dove. I tried to catch it but it evaded me. Someone shackled my wrists. Without my hands, I ran through the room behind the Qur'an. It flew into my mother's room, and I stumbled and followed it at a crawl. As soon as my head entered the room, I fell into darkness. My cheek fell on the tip of a military boot. It smelled foul. The boot kicked me. A hand dragged me upwards by my long beard and I came face to face with the same giant man swathed in black. His eyes were flashing sparks. He hit me twice in the face with his crotch, rubbed it against my face, then took his long penis out from behind the black and forced it in my mouth until it reached the top of my stomach. Foam spurted out of my mouth and all over the ground. He was still choking me with his rigid penis. Dozens of black-clothed men gathered round, all photocopies of each other. I couldn't shout—he had jammed my throat with his cock. One of them tore my trousers and shoved his dick inside me. I wanted to bite down on the cock that clogged my mouth, but it was like iron. All the men threw their heavy bodies on top of me and fucked me without pause. I couldn't breathe, the metal penis was blocking my throat. I pushed the man away with all my strength so I could catch my breath. The penis came out from the sheath of my throat and the man fell backwards. His penis was a drawn sword, covered in blood. I gasped.

I took my hand out of my pants. It had been gripping my rock-hard erection as if it were an iron dildo. The Arabic language teacher had never mentioned that my worst fears could fuck me in my dreams. My fingers were stuck together with sticky, warm fluid. I wiped my hand on the hem of my shirt. For the thousandth time I opened my bag and gazed at the mangled stumps of the red Qur'an. I couldn't bear to look for more than a second. It seemed to have eyes, and I was terrified of meeting them. It was starting to look like my death warrant ... my expulsion from this place ... my imprisonment ... like photos of me in newspapers and magazines ... a terrorist fleeing justice. That is what would happen if someone looked in my bag. The terrorist video and the red Qur'an had had more than a million views in less than twenty-four hours. How many people in this very building had seen it? How many times had Swedish television showed it? How could they believe I had no connection to this murderer? How had it ended up in my bag? Would they understand what it meant to me? Would they believe the love story between the red Qur'an and my mother? What if the Immigration Bureau uncovered the red Qur'an in my possession? They would never believe me, however much I swore I wasn't the murderer. Everyone would testify against me, just to exonerate themselves. That night was longer than the whole journey on foot from Greece to Austria.

Carrying my bag with the remnants of the red Qur'an inside it, I ran into the forest. I hurried between the trees, running and walking and running again while steam puffed from my nose and mouth, until I reached the lake.

I looked over my shoulder to check no one was watching me as I dug a hole in the ground, then I opened the bag like I was tearing a winding sheet, took out the pages and the hard cover of the red Qur'an, and placed them all in the pit. I took a lighter out of my pocket and set fire to the pages. The tongues of flame soon swallowed up the pages of the red Qur'an, which made a crackling sound as they burned. These were the first burial rites I had undertaken in my life.

CHAPTER 7

On the Edge of Madness

Avoid eating these poisonous mushrooms

The title of this Arabic leaflet brought me to a halt. It was in a rack in the waiting room of the Immigration Bureau, hanging above the waiting heads buried in their phones. I was walking towards the pamphlet to read its contents when one of the women called my name. "Furat?" I turned around and saw a young-looking girl, tall and extremely thin, clutching a pile of papers and standing in the middle of the room. At the same moment my phone vibrated in my hand. The name of one of my brothers in Syria appeared on the screen. The girl continued saying my name in a halting manner, apparently spelling it out loud. *Layla is dead.* I gulped down this poisonous news from my brother in silence. I hid Layla's corpse in my trouser pocket and rubbed my hands together as if I was washing the blood off. "Hello, I am the interviewer. Follow me to the meeting room," the woman told me, staring at my thick black beard.

Layla was the only daughter of my mother's sister. She hadn't yet finished her high school education when she decided to be my aunt's right hand in the kitchen, but before long she met a Kurdish man from Amouda when his military service brought him to Deir Ezzor. He saw her for the first time at the coffee grinder's when he was buying coffee for the officer whose house he was guarding, and he instantly fell in love with the fresh, blooming face peering out from her white hijab as she opened the paper bag of fresh coffee beans. His enraptured gaze became entangled in her plump white fingers and her red nails as she settled up with the grinder. When she left, he followed her, watching the curves of her short, full body inside her floral corduroy dress as she strutted in time to the melodies of the local mawwal songs. He left without buying any coffee and followed Layla until he had worked out where her family home was. That day Layla earned him a three-day stay in jail for failing to bring the coffee to his officer in time. As soon as his punishment was up, he went straight from his cell to my aunt's house and asked for Layla's hand in marriage. Despite my aunt's initial objections—she didn't want to lose the help in the kitchen—they got married after a year-long engagement, which was the remaining period of his military service.

I remember their wedding well, a folk carnival held in front of my aunt's house in our neighbourhood. The groom's family were bussed over from Amouda, accompanied by drums and a mizmar. There was dancing, and a dabke line for whomever wanted it, and tables of baklawa and kunafa filled my aunt's garden. Layla was hidden inside an enormous white satin dress. She had placed a tiara on top of her hijab like a princess and made up her face in dazzling colours. The women flocked around her and hung gold jewellery over her hands, fingers, and neck, and they kissed her one after another like a Mesopotamian goddess. The groom stood beside her like a hawk. He squared his broad shoulders and stuck out his chest beneath his cream-coloured suit while a wine-coloured bow tie gleamed around his neck. He had parted his hair at the side and shaved his beard and waxed his cheeks until they were red as chard, but he let his flourishing moustache cover his upper lip. His wide eyes sparkled in the middle of his round face. I never forgot the sight of his thickset finger when Layla put a chunky golden ring around it, and the long nail of his little finger.

The guests showered Layla and her groom with gold liras and sweets and chocolate wrapped in colourful paper, while I and the other neighbourhood children threw ourselves among their feet and scrabbled to collect them from the ground—my hands were too small to hold everything, so I held the hem of my shirt like a kangaroo's pocket and filled it with coins and sweets. That was Layla's last night in Deir Ezzor. The Kurds carried her and her bridegroom off in a procession to Amouda a few hours after the wedding, leaving a multi-coloured sea of cellophane-wrapped sweets behind them. After that, Layla opened our door to the world of the Kurds, which had been a mystery to us. Our annual visits to Layla in Amouda became a much-loved summer ritual for our family. We would stay in her countryside house, and she would bake thick bread in the tannour and cook chicken with bulgur wheat over the coals. If there was no wedding to attend in the area, she and her husband would take us to the fields of wheat and barley in the evening where we would perch on tall iron camp beds to be out of reach of scorpions, and when we grew tired of laughing, we would lie on our backs and doze off, counting the stars in the sky. Layla became pregnant after more than a decade of trying. And because our customs force young widows to return to their father's house, Layla returned to Deir Ezzor still pregnant, after the security services blew her husband's head off during a riot at a football game in Qamishli.

When Layla returned to Deir Ezzor as a widow, my aunt was initially overjoyed that her right hand had returned to her kitchen. But both of Layla's arms were occupied by the baby who cried all day long. Layla had to pick him up and walk with him all through the house and garden. Before long, Layla and her son grew to be a burden on my aunt and the whole house. My aunt wanted to marry her off again and suggested various widowers, divorcés, and old men—but Layla refused them all. She wanted to dedicate her life to raising her son. She desperately wanted to go back to Amouda where her son was born and where her husband's grave lay, but her father wouldn't allow it.

A slender girl was waiting for us at the door of the room. The interviewer introduced her by saying, "She's the interpreter—she is obligated to ensure everything you say remains confidential," before inviting me to go inside. The room was large, cold, and damp, and everything inside it was grey. It was like a grave under construction. At the end stood a large, immaculately clean desk with nothing on it apart from a computer keyboard. Behind the desk was a swivel chair, and next to it was a chair for the translator, and in front of it was a confessional chair—which, of course, was mine. The room had a large window that looked out at a cement wall, graffitied over with a picture of Layla in her wedding dress. The interviewer asked me to sit then turned away and took her own seat behind the desk. With her black blazer and neatly combed blonde hair, she looked like a newsreader on one of the foreign channels. On her left, the translator was wearing a tight black jumpsuit that showed off her beautiful figure, the V-shaped neck baring part of her round, white breasts. She was wearing full makeup and hadn't forgotten to stick on false eyelashes; she looked as though she were on her way to a dinner party. In her lap she had placed her small, black handbag that displayed a Chanel logo in gilded metal, clearly an imitation. The handle dangled over her legs, a fine leather strip threaded through the gold chain. One leg twisted around the other like a serpent, and the ends of her long, loose black hair just about brushed the points on her stiletto heels. She greeted me in an accent that didn't belong to any Arab country. I sat on the edge of my confessional chair in the middle of the room while Layla's body twitched in my pocket. The opening silence was interrupted by a lament from my stomach, upset by the poisonous news I had swallowed, and the interviewer's fingers tapping on the keyboard as she typed out each letter of my name. "Please look at the interviewer's face only, and listen to the Arabic translation with your ears only," the interpreter said.

Ibn Layla—Layla's son. That was how he was known to our family and everyone in the neighbourhood, to the point that we forgot his actual name. This Kurdish child was brought up among Arabs, with a mother who spoke to him only in Kurdish, a language she had mastered thanks to the child's father. He was a carbon copy of Layla with his thick, black curly hair, his round white face, and his black eyes. Layla would always cover him with the end of her scarf as he curled his legs around her right hip. She used to say, "He isn't just my son, he is part of me." Layla was terrified of anything happening to him, and even a passing breeze would alarm her; he was raised on her hip, clinging to her like a koala. The revolution broke out in Deir Ezzor in the same year that Layla's son started primary school. He was enrolled in the neighbourhood school my siblings and I, and Layla herself, had attended. Layla took him by the hand every day on the way to the school gate, and for the next five hours she waited for him on the pavement until class was over.

One scorching morning, after a night of intense fighting, the smell of gunpowder still hung warm in the air. The ground was riddled with empty bullet casings, and car chases had left black tyre marks on the asphalt. Layla kissed her son's hand at the school gate and let him go inside with the other pupils.

A few minutes later an aeroplane hovered overhead, fired three missiles at the school, and followed up by bombing the neighbouring houses. Layla shredded her dress, ripped off her hijab and tore at her loose hair. She pressed her hands against her chest as she let out a scream that vanished inside a cloud of cement dust. Her son was pulled from underneath the rubble looking like a tiny cement statue, still wearing his backpack. Layla clutched him to her, draping his legs around her waist and wrapping him in her arms so his face was pressed to her uncovered chest. She hid his face with her hijab and ran barefoot towards the banks of the Euphrates with dozens of others, bombs raining down all the while. She joined a group of other terrified people and hurled herself inside a small tin boat that was heading to the north bank, the only means of crossing the river after all the bridges had been destroyed. The terrified passengers had to stay on the dusty bank until a bus was able to take them somewhere less dangerous. A warm, sticky night fell, and the scared passengers lay down on the riverside, their eyes open like carp for sale. All except for Layla, who slept standing up, her son draped over her hip and his head still covered with her hijab.

Eventually, dawn stung people's faces. They started complaining about a strange smell. Layla tucked more of her hijab over her son's head. The group started to split up and some of them plunged into the river and began splashing their faces to alleviate the oppressive heat. The smell clung to Layla's hip as she circulated the group, trying to convince them there was no smell at all. The frightened women encircled her and slowly stepped towards her until they surrounded her on all sides. Layla sat down, her masked son in her lap, and thrust her toes into the soil. The shadows of the women's bodies concealed her face. She lay down on the ground and began to dig a hollow with her head, and another with her feet, and a grave for her back. Her plump breasts were exposed, trembling on top of her white chest, displaying her brown nipples. She squeezed her eyelids shut and thrust her son into her stomach, and the women found their faces scorched by the blazing heat of her screams, as if she had given birth to him all over again. She drew blood from the arms that plucked the child away from her womb, lashing out with nails stuffed with cement. Ibn Layla's body had begun to decay, as they saw when they dangled him by his feet in the air.

The group let Layla scatter soil over her bare flesh in the middle of the women. They recited funeral prayers over her son then buried him in his school uniform, there on the riverbank. They left her his backpack.

"Four months ago, when you give fingerprints and make your asylum claim, you said you are, um, one of those who likes boys, yes? You stick to that?" The girl interpreted the interviewer's perspective while passing her beautifully manicured crimson nails through her hair. It was the first time in my life someone was asking me to define my identity. How could I talk about my sexuality for the first time? I couldn't really understand what the interpreter was saying, but she seemed very serious.

A year after her son's murder, Layla accompanied me to the north-westerly tip of Syria. We had an appointment with one of her husband's relatives who was working as a smuggler. We waited for him in the middle of an abundant cornfield. Turkey lay before us, lit by the afternoon sun. Beyond the bare hill lay Mardin, where both our mothers had been born. She and I mulled over our memories while we waited, never opening our mouths. There was a bleak silence, as though the earth had stopped turning. Layla swivelled her emaciated frame and folded up her bones inside the loose black fabric of her burka, settling on the dust like a rose tossed onto a grave. She wasn't the Layla I had known; *the lioness*, we used to call her. Now, she was more like a stray gazelle. Through the slit in her dark niqab, her eyelashes fluttered in the hollows of her emptied eyes. My scrutiny of her face was interrupted by the sound of an approaching motorbike. I smiled at her, and she read fear in my smile. She looked into my eyes and reached out a hand covered in black cotton; with a tenderness that kept my heart going, she settled her hand in mine. Her muffled voice slipped out from beneath the niqab. "If you go back, you'll fall into our madness. If you go forwards, you'll throw yourself into the madness of others. Right now, you're on the edge of madness and you have to choose which one you want to fall into."

Layla's body lay in my pocket, and my guts were slowly being poisoned.

"The interview is finished," said the girl's voice.

CHAPTER 8

Thieves' Market

Abu Gharam

Our darkened room was filled with a woman's moans and gasps, punctuated by the heavy breathing of a man whispering words I didn't understand. The woman's sighs accelerated to the rhythm of flesh hitting flesh. The heat in the room was overwhelming, and the bed was blazing beneath me. My behind curved and swelled like a hemispherical shell, like I was a snail whose slimy stomach was stuck to the bed. The woman's gasps reached a climax and the man's breaths grew louder. Then the sound suddenly cut off.

My roommate sighed under his blanket, loud enough that his orgasm couldn't be heard over his exhalation, then he fell silent. I kept quiet, pretending to be asleep in my bed, which was directly beneath his. I stifled my breathing in the pillow and cautiously listened for the shuffle of his hand as he pulled it over his coarse pubic hair and away from his crotch. I listened intently to the sound of his underwear elastic snapping over his skin. A gust of heat hit my bare back like a live coal, and I realised he had raised the blanket away from his burning body. "Astaghfirullah," he sighed with a hint of guilt. I heard his phone beep four times. "A'ouz bi-Allah min ash-Shaitan Al-Rajim..." A dulcet recitation of the Qur'an sounded from the phone. The reciter's voice was muffled when my roommate fell asleep, and his breathing became increasingly raspy. A few moments later, his limp hand fell out of the upper bunk and swung over my head like a hanged man. Quietly, I turned over to lie on my back. I pulled the cover up away from my hips and fell asleep to the sound of his breathing.

This scene was my lullaby every night in the refugee's building. We were now alone in the apartment which everyone else had left once the decision about their residency had been made. My roommate's nickname was Abu Gharam; I could never remember his real name, although I knew it from helping to translate his letters from the Immigration Bureau. Abu Gharam used to sleep right on top of me, that is, in the top bunk, because our wooden beds were in layers to fit the narrow dimensions of the room. Abu Gharam was over forty, but he had the muscles of a teenager, and his bulging veins made his body look like it was bound with ropes. His fingers were long and spindly, and his nails were always pared and clean, but he had let the nail of the little finger on his right hand grow long and sharp as a knife. His wheat-coloured forehead was broad and spacious, and his black, widely-spaced eyebrows curved like a drawn sword over each eye. His sleepy eyes made his face look gentle, even familiar. He had a tall, slender frame like a mast, and he walked like a sail blown by the wind. His chest was so hairy it reached all the way up to his beard, but his back was smooth and bore a vividly coloured, somewhat blurry tattoo. His arms were covered with scars, as though he had tried to cut a vein for every year of his life.

Abu Gharam was constantly grumbling about the heat and the radiators, especially at night. He could only remain in bed if he was half-naked, uncovering his long, hairy legs. He was a branch broken off its tree, and appeared to have no family or anyone who was worried about him. His wife divorced him in 2006 after she tasted alcohol on his breath. She deprived him of his only child with a court judgement, and after the son suckled the milk of hatred from his mother, he chose to stay with her once he was older. After the divorce, Abu Gharam spent his life looking after his elderly mother until her death. His siblings sold the family home in Harasta, so he rented a furnished room in the Dweil'a neighbourhood in southern Damascus, where penniless men, soldiers, and students lived in shared houses. Abu Gharam was tainted by stigma because of his work in Souk Al-Haramiya—the Thieves' Market—as a trader and repairer of used mobile phones. Harassment from Assad's men had forced him to flee the country. "At the end of the day they'd bring fifteen mobile phones they'd nicked from the checkpoints during their so-called searches, and they insisted I buy them or they'd burn down my shop." He told me about the trucks that arrived from Rif Dimashq and Homs carrying furnishings, fridges, and washing machines, all stolen from people's homes by Assad's soldiers after their inhabitants had fled the bombings. Abu Gharam's Harastani accent helped me imagine the way he spoke to cunning hawkers in the middle of the market crowds.

Souk Al-Haramiya was run exclusively by men, and it lay between Al-Thawra Street and Al-Nasr Street in downtown Damascus. Its twists and turns were filled with used furniture piled so high that they formed bridges in some places. Hundreds of wooden doors leaned against walls of damaged, bare blocks in between piles of used clothing and a series of cooking pots with scorched bottoms and broken handles. The aroma of roasted meat wafted from its small restaurants and mingled with coffee, fermented tea, boiled fuul, chickpeas, and corn on the cob. Shards of porcelain, none of which resembled any of the others, were strewn everywhere, along with broken bits of furniture scattered left and right along the length of the market pavements. A sofa arm or a chair leg, the head of a broken doll, or a doll's bare trunk without feet. A single child's trainer. A watch with only one strap. Idle ceiling fans. Electrical appliances, smashed mobile phones. It was like the aftermath of the bombings you see on the news. But it was just a market for second-hand goods, without any corpses.

Souk Al-Haramiya had its own particular laws unlike those of the other markets in the city. What was sold there could not be returned or exchanged—you bought the goods at your own risk, what was known as "sale at sea." The souk had been given its name by the inhabitants of Damascus because in the past it used to be the place where thieves and pickpockets showcased their wares. But as the years passed it turned into a large, regulated market for appliances and used furniture; every day dozens of traders worked there, and thousands of people patronised it.

Abu Gharam often told me about his daily life in Souk Al-Haramiya, especially during the war. He told me many Damascenes denied ever having sold their furniture there with the intention of fleeing to Europe. His speech was peppered with phrases from the street hawkers who roamed in front of the blankets loaded with scrap and trinkets. And as his hands flew about gesturing, they released the scent of the men's bodies in Hammam Al-Khanji, close by Souk Al-Haramiya. At the end of each day, this large hammam filled up with traders and clients from the market, along with bus drivers and taxi drivers. They went there to sluice their bodies with hot water and laurel soap, relax, and then peel an orange or mandarin to eat in the steam room. Then the men would lie on their backs in the shadowy niches. I, along with many other gay men, headed there to meet them. The patrons of Hammam Al-Khanji were the most relaxed when it came to gay men, freely and comfortably handing their bared upper bodies over to us. It didn't stop there—I felt safe with them so I would talk about whatever was in my mind, and together we would discuss the importance of feeling free in your body, being comfortable undressed. We talked about individual liberty and the stigma of shame that society stamped on those it disapproved of, even though they had committed no sin. Some hadn't finished their education and had no preconceived notions about being gay. The men working in Souk Al-Haramiya were also branded for crimes they hadn't committed, but inside themselves they were free. They were merely victims of society, these penniless men trading in second-hand odds and ends.

Abu Gharam told me his past in Damascus was confined to the walls of Souk Al-Haramiya. He couldn't form friendships with anyone outside the market—the whiff of *thief* stuck to him and everyone who worked there. However, he had a very different experience in the asylboende—his skill at buying and selling and chatting with clients made him popular among asylum seekers. He spent most of his time helping them to mend or update their smartphones, using his long sharp nail as a tool to open up the phone. He himself used an ancient Nokia Teardrop. He went out every morning and only came back to sleep—he used the room like a hotel. After three months of sharing a room with him, I was certain all he had on his phone was a short porn film and a surah from the Qur'an to cleanse himself of the guilt of having watched it.

That was all I knew about him.

Every morning, I made sure to wipe up all the yellow spots of urine Abu Gharam was in the habit of leaving on the toilet rim before I took off all my clothes, sat on the toilet, and opened the front-facing camera on my phone to use it like a hand mirror. I reached my finger down from above, pressed the middle of my forehead, and pulled up my forehead and eyebrows. *Do I need Botox?* I didn't have this beard when I visited Hammam Al-Khanji—I was smooth-skinned then. I began to inspect my chest and the bits of my body visible on my screen. Was my chest hairier than it used to be? I didn't recognise my skin, it seemed dry. I didn't believe it was the effect of age. Just like I was missing myself, my soul longed for its dressing ... it missed my body. I hadn't checked in with my body since arriving in this forest. I shut off the camera, opened my private notebook, and poured out my feelings about Abu Gharam.

I'm not sure if it's love or lust or friendship I feel. But his smell, his character, and our conversations remind me of my sexual past in Damascus. All of this confusion and contradiction between us makes me yearn to embrace him, to fall asleep with him, without sin or guilt.

The Soul's Longing for the Body

I put my backpack on like a snail's shell, and began contracting and unfurling towards Småland's dense forests. I only stopped when I reached my favourite point—my smultronställe. This was a large grey boulder with a wide, flat surface which looked a little like a bed. It was surrounded by a delicate stream of water, concealed beneath grass, weeds, and fallen tree branches. Only the gurgle of water broke the quiet. Towering pine trees enveloped the site, blocking out the sunlight and creating a room. I took off my shell and put it down at my side. Piece by piece, I tossed my clothes all around me—I threw my underwear up in the air and didn't see where it landed. I opened my bag and took out the bar of laurel soap I had bought from an Arabic shop, and I held it as though it were a butterfly that had alighted on the tips of my fingers. I lay on my back and let my skin stick to the protuberances of the rock. The pine trees swayed towards me to get a better look. I lowered my fingertips into the little stream, sprinkled a little water over my body, and rubbed the laurel soap over it. I took the slickness of the soap and rubbed it over my neck and chest, under my armpits, over my stomach, until I reached my crotch and thighs, repeating this action whenever the water dried over my body, as if carefully irrigating parched earth. Finally, I closed my eyes and listened to the twittering birds and inhaled the scent of pine blended with the soap on my body. I tumbled to the bottom of my memories and saw myself, the midwife dangling me by the feet—I laughed and cried simultaneously on my mother's breast. I saw my mother's hand stroking my head, washing it with a piece of soap bigger than my head itself. I saw my clothes, neatly arranged in my wardrobe in Damascus, a tiny piece of soap hanging in between them to keep them smelling nice. I saw a piece of soap in the crystal shell on the washbasin of my family home.

I was woken by a sudden movement nearby—apparently a bird had taken flight. Picking up my notebook from my bag, I added this phrase into my notes about Abu Gharam. *I wish it had been Abu Gharam and not a bird ... If only he had followed me to the forest to sneak a look at my naked body from behind the pine trees.*

I took out a razor blade, a water bottle, and a towel, then steadied my phone in front of me on the rock and opened the camera so it reflected my long beard. *Time to shave.*

I moistened my beard with the water and began to rub soap into it until it foamed, then smeared the foam around until it covered my chest and spread all the way under my armpits, across my stomach, my pubic hair, and my bottom. I put the razor blade to my beard and didn't put it down until my reflection in the phone screen appeared smooth and soft, just the way the men in Hammam Al-Khanji liked it. I took a few photos of my body in its soft new guise, in poses that left my sexual desire in absolutely no doubt. I decided to go back to the asylboende and give my phone to Abu Gharam to update it, on the pretext that my phone memory had no more space for photos.

The Body's Longing for the Soul

"It's boiling tonight, I can't sleep with anything on," Abu Gharam said, lying in bed. I was also lying in bed, directly beneath him, my naked body hidden beneath a blanket. I thought he and his bed were going to collapse on my head when he shifted his body with a deep sigh. His underwear dropped onto the end of my bed, next to my head. I didn't push them to the floor—I let them stay there. Abu Gharam rasped his nails against his chest. I sent him a sigh in return. The heat of the room was overwhelming. In the darkness, his hand dangled off the bed like a vine seeking something to cling to. I raised my arm like a wary snake that caught the hard stem in its mouth. Soon, the branch blossomed a hand that writhed over my arm. Abu Gharam descended from above like rain.

He accepted my invitation with a smile, and we embraced like a pair of branches in springtime. He held me to his broad chest in a gesture that sent a wave of tenderness through me, tenderness I hadn't felt since arriving in Sweden. I tried to turn my back towards him so he could enter me, but he steadied my face firmly and brought it towards him until our noses were touching. His breath was warm on my face. I became aware of his body's deep longing for his soul, similar to mine. A tear made its way down his cheek. I embraced him lovingly and, like a blind man, used my fingers to read the tragedy of scars on his forearms. We were a pile of pain and yearning, crying on each other's chests. He put his hand on my heart from the back and drew me towards him, pulling me close as though he hoped I would enter his own heart. I clung to his back and pushed my hands upwards until I encircled his neck and my fingers were playing with the ends of his hair, then kept going until my whole hands were plunged into his thick hair. He rested his sweaty forehead against mine. I sank my face between the side of his chest and my bed, and a rush of sobs came over me. I tasted his salty tears on my lips. We cried as we had never cried in our lives. We were sobbing, our scorching tears fusing our faces until their features blurred and vanished. We wept Damascus, we wept Ghouta, we wept Deir Ezzor, we wept Aleppo. We wept our streets, and we wept Souk Al-Haramiya. We wept hammams and laurel soap, we wept orchards and gardens, we wept the Euphrates and its loss. We wept our waste and wandering, our goodbyes and arrivals, we wept the sea, we wept the land. We wept the shade of apricot trees, we wept the taste of oranges, we wept mountains of watermelons. We wept poverty, we wept injustice, our weakness, the heart of Damascus. We wept the revolution. We wept the war, we wept shame, we wept tyranny, we wept because we were Syrians. We wept our morning breakfasts and our evening gatherings. We wept our dead. We wept our mothers, fathers, children, sisters and brothers. We wept the past, the present, the future. We wept fear, despair, loneliness and separation. We wept our homes. We wept our doors, our beds, our pillows. We wept distance. We wept because we were still alive and we wept because we were already dead.

CHAPTER 9

Fabric Memory

It was my last day in the asylboende. I soaked my naked body in a spot of April sunshine that was falling onto my bed. Piled up all around me were clothes I had bought from various second-hand shops throughout Småland. I had forgotten how to pack a suitcase—I had become the kind of person more used to fleeing at short notice than packing up in advance.

Your memory is fabric, Furat. It is disappearing behind the curtains of the bedrooms that have been gutted by fires in the war. It is sitting on the tablecloths that kitchen ceilings have fallen in on. Your memory is like a suitcase, overflowing with the dresses and shirts that the security agents tossed on the ground like bodies without souls after ransacking the wardrobes. Remember lying your head on the soft pillow that your mother's own hands sewed and stuffed with feathers and lavender. Write about clothes and fabric, Furat, seeing as you haven't yet! Who will remember the vaulted fabric market of Deir Ezzor now that it's been burned to the ground? Or Souk Al-Hamidiyah and the windows of the fabric shops? Write about cloth, Furat. Write about how you disappeared inside white bedsheets pulled off your mother's bed, how you wrapped them around your small body and paraded about like a little Greek boy, showing off and dancing for your mother and making her eyes vanish from laughing so hard. Write about the clothes that you left behind in Damascus like orphans. Write about the military uniform you rejected when you refused to fight against your people, the cotton pyjamas you left on the floor when you rushed out of your house in a panic between hails of bullets. Write about your shoes whose leather was eaten up by sea salt, write about how your escape tore them to shreds. Write, Furat, because you survived the fire that took people and stone and cloth as its fuel. Write, because it is your duty to tell their stories.

This monologue swirled around my head as I picked up my belongings, folded them, and put them in my bag. I recited these clothes as if they had been written long ago. It isn't fair to write about the people I met on my journey and not about the cloth that clung to my skin along the way and kept watch every night. As soon as I decided to tell the tales of the clothes that I wore to leave Syria, and which I was wearing when I arrived in Sweden, the second-hand clothes gathered around me like children, impatient to hear the stories about their kin.

The Small White Sock

Last night in Damascus, Hayy al-Muhajireen

The last place I rented in Damascus was a tiny place in Hayy al-Muhajireen on the western slope of Mount Qasioun. It formed part of a grand Damascene villa that was about a century old. Hayy Al-Muhajireen, the Migrant's Quarter—the name was like the mark I bear now as I tell my story. My house was surrounded by presidential palaces and the houses of state officials and ambassadors who had all fled because of the war. This district was supposedly the safest place in Damascus at that time, but I felt as though I were in direct contact with terror. Black-uniformed guards were everywhere, guns poking out of the back of their trousers. I still see images of that old quarter, the people's frightened faces, the eyes of the informers that scanned passersby with fingers ready to secretly pull the trigger. I remember how people stepped cautiously as though they were walking backwards; I remember the disciplined motion of their arms, afraid that any free movement or spontaneous gesture could cast them into the unknown.

My bedroom window looked out over Damascus. I used to drive up Mount Qasioun in the evenings just to enjoy the view as the city transformed into a handful of pearls, an illuminated carnival of colours—now, I didn't even dare look out of my own window. I was afraid of seeing Damascus oppressed and grieving.

I spent most of my time under the blanket in my bedroom, especially when the electricity was cut off for hours at a time. One such evening I was lying on my bed, a huge, ornate brass affair that dated back to the French Occupation. I rested my head on the pink pillow embroidered with a line of Omar Khayyam: *Sleep has not lengthened the life of any, nor has any life been shortened by nightlong revels.* The room was lit by three candles, their flames trembling from cold. I closed my fist around my phone and fixed a wide-eyed stare on the ceiling, meditating on the thick wooden beams. My phone buzzed in my hand and I raised my arm and held the screen over my face. It was a text from my cousin Layla: *Come to Qamishli and leave the rest to me.* It was a clear, indisputable invitation to help me escape to Turkey. I read the message three times, then leaned the phone next to my head. I pulled my shoulders underneath the blanket and left my head and stubbled face outside. *Is my love story with Damascus over? Damascus has started to frighten me.* I sat up in bed, facing the long, thin window covered by white laced curtains. Before darkness fell I had closed the window—without locking it, as instructed by the landlady, so the century-old stained glass wouldn't be shattered if a bomb went off outside. She was anxious about every little piece of her house and insisted I be careful even while walking on the Ottoman flooring because every piece was an *original*—she was certain that in the future, her home would become a museum of the historical Damascene house.

Silhouettes of the branches from the neighbours' bitter orange tree, heavily laden with fruit, could be seen from my window. Its leaves stuck to the outside of the windowpane like eyes watching me. The walls of the room were painted light green. To my right, a wooden wardrobe inlaid with mother-of-pearl covered the entire wall. On the opposite wall were wooden shelves decorated with brass where I had put some simple French novels intended for beginners and the complete writings of Ghada Samman in Arabic. If it wasn't for Ghada and her words, what would I have done on those long lonely nights? And there was also a suitcase, clad in brown leather that had been worked and embroidered with gold thread, containing a Qur'an from Mecca. It was about seventy years old and belonged to the landlady.

Suddenly a light from outside streamed onto the ceiling, causing the shadows of the bitter orange tree leaves to climb upwards and grow over my body and face, then carry on up the wall and across the ceiling, before retreating and descending over the books. From outside came the sound of car tyres crawling over the gravel. I got up from the bed and tiptoed barefoot over the square tiles. I stood in the middle of the room. The car engine stopped running. The sound of the car door opening and closing. Heavy footsteps and the jangling of keys, the sound of the key sliding in the lock. Knocking on the door. The door creaking open. The wooden door closing.

All quiet. And I was still standing in the middle of the room like I was onstage, holding my head in my hands, trying to work out what had happened.

From all around I suddenly heard applause and the yells of the neighbourhood kids. The electricity had returned. Life returned to Damascus. I briefly scrutinised the plant reliefs carved onto the brass candlestick, a lizard trying to scale a blossoming branch. It was a work of art. I blew out all three candles, one after another, and opened the window to let out the smell of wax and let in the lights from the neighbouring houses. I grabbed a branch of the bitter orange tree and pulled it inside the room, letting it dangle so it brushed against the branches traced on the floor. Struck with sudden courage, I leaned my head outside so I was facing Damascus from behind the bitter orange tree, and I read out my final letter to her:

My dearest Damascus,

It has been the greatest honour and pleasure of my life that you chose me as one of the last to live in your alleyways. I will keep some of your beauty in my memory, and I will carry the legacy of your features before the niqab dropped over your mutilated face.

Thank you, Damascus.

I let the branch spring back and shut the window quietly. A leaf from the bitter orange tree fell on the floor. I picked it up off the ground, along with *The Other Time of Love*, and gently lay the leaf between the words of Ghada Samman on page 62:

"I decided to escape into the street. And when I opened my wardrobe to put some clothes on, my tragedy appeared before me, hanging down the length of clothes ... my surprising clothes ... half of them simple like a naïve schoolgirl's, clinging to clothes that were sparkling, vividly colourful, bare-shouldered, befitting a vivacious *actrice*! My clothes are an irreconcilable, impossible contradiction. Perhaps they engage in violent clashes when I close the wardrobe door—the schoolgirl clothes would like to murder the actress clothes that struggle fiercely, then they all scurry back to their places when they hear my footsteps in the room ... which of these clothes belong to me? Which to wear?"

I put my hand inside my wardrobe and emptied all its contents onto the ground. Then I opened the biggest suitcase I owned, made of real leather with a huge gold-plated lock. My grandmother used it to hold bolts of rare, silver-embroidered fabric; I inherited the suitcase from her after the fabric was distributed among my mother and my aunts, and she asked me to hold onto it because she had bought it in Mardin before she moved to Deir Ezzor with my grandfather.

I tossed my clothes into the suitcase, piece by piece. Each one of them was a costume from a scene of my life in Damascus. They all ended up piled in suitcases like so many prisoners in isolation, watching me balefully. "I can't take you all with me, I don't know the way and it will be a long journey. I am sorry, my dear, dear friends—it will be a long wait for us." I spotted a small white sock, curled up like a small, frightened mouse hiding in the furthest corner of the wardrobe. It was my sock, from when I was six. My mother had kept it and used to hang it on her wardrobe door in her bedroom. She gave it back to me as a gift on my thirtieth birthday.

I scooped up the sock from the furthest corner of the wardrobe and embraced it. It smelled of my mother's wardrobe. The next moment, I was sitting on my tall wooden chair in our sunny kitchen and my mother was kneeling in front of me trying to put this very sock on me, apologising because all she bought me for Eid al-Adha were these socks. I would be wearing the same clothes I did for Eid al-Fitr because things had been hard for our family since the death of my father.

"Don't be sad, yabny. Nothing stays the same, everything changes eventually. Look at your little feet—they won't stay that size forever! And not just your shoe size. Everything changes, yabny, and nothing stays as it is. The day we are living right now will be in the past by tomorrow. So don't be sad if we have some rough times. You can be sure one day it will all be in the past."

I decided to take my mother's philosophy with me on my journey. As if I was hiding a gold ring, I hid the small sock in an inner pocket of my rucksack. I locked the suitcase, left it in the corner of the room, and threw the clothes I wanted to travel in on top: a flannel shirt with red and blue checks, and comfortable, loose, navy cotton trousers with many pockets and strong zips. I turned off the light and slipped under the blanket.

The sound of an explosion woke me the next morning. The force of it blew the window open on its hinges. The tree branches were blown inside my room. Gunshots rang out nearby. I put the pillow over my head, threw myself on the ground and rolled under the bed where I found a massacred bitter orange. I pressed the fruit to my heart, and the perfume of Damascus flowed from its wounds. The gunfire outside intensified. Ambulances and fire engines blasted their sirens. I heard footsteps running in the alley and the neighbours whispering to each other through their skylights. Another explosion rocked the bed and three more oranges fell to the floor.

I inhaled the dust on the painted tiles, the smell of the gunpowder and smoke and the scent of the thick fruits as they rolled over in agony. I realised the floor was listing from time—it sloped towards me so my frightened body became the endpoint, and everything that fell on the ground would roll in my direction. Under the bed I discovered I shared the room with a kingdom unto itself, one with its own queen, soldiers, and workers. Ants had taken no notice of the landlady's fear for her *authentic* Ottoman tiles and had gnawed their way underneath, making them into a roof for their kingdom.

The last time I hid under the bed by myself was in Deir Ezzor when I was nine years old and terrified of my big brother because I had thrown his ball in the Euphrates and the current had swept it away. I remember being like a frightened kitten when he gently pulled me out. He sat down next to me and said he had forgiven me, and the ball had probably carried on swimming all the way to Iraq. And they would be really happy the ball had got there, especially as they were going through a war and a siege. He told me about the unique position I enjoyed among my siblings because my name was Furat, named after the river of our city, the River Furat—the Euphrates. He told me about all the people with my name and said I would share many of the river's virtues. The river travelled from Turkey without tiring and entered Syria without papers because it believed in freedom; it watered everywhere equally, making no distinction between a small town and a large city, and then it carried on its journey to Iraq, ignoring the dispute between Saddam Hussein and Hafez Assad. The Euphrates believed someone was always waiting for it. Rebellious and powerful, it never paused until it reached the sea, which it plunged into full of courage, without fear of the salt.

While I was hiding under the bed, my distant memories calmed my fears. My mind started telling stories to my heart to drive out the terror. Perhaps this is the only way of living with fear. If I was to complete my journey, travelling in the opposite direction to the Euphrates, my memory would be my saviour in moments of fear and loneliness.

The shooting outside stopped. I emerged from my trench, crawling on my stomach. I took off my thin cotton pyjamas, threw them on the floor, then kicked them under the bed along with my pillow and the bitter orange fruit. In a panic I took the flannel shirt and put it on, thrust my legs inside the navy-blue trousers, pushed my feet into my honey-brown boots, snatched up the red rucksack, and left for Abbasid Bus Station to take the first bus heading northeast towards Qamishli.

According to state TV, an assault on the Army Staff Headquarters in Umayyad Square had been carried out by armed insurgents that day. According to the revolution's network, a group from the Free Army decided to gain control of the Army HQ in the capital, along with the Syrian Television and Radio Building next door.

The taxi had to stop a kilometre from the bus station because of the checkpoints. I got out and set off on foot with hundreds of others who were also leaving Damascus. The hourglass of Syria had flipped and we were all like sand streaming through the narrow bottleneck. The anticipation ... Perhaps someone would come and turn it over again, and we would all fall back into the place we had escaped from.

The Red-and-Blue-Checked Shirt

Damascus, Autumn 2010

It wasn't easy to fold this shirt. It lay heavily in my hands. I let it slump in my lap and put my palms on top, feeling the flannel, delicate and tender all at once, brave and robust, stitched with warm and painful memories. I stuck my thumb inside and poked it out through the hole in the middle of the back. Syrians always talk about the holes the barbed wire left in the backs of their clothes. It seems we all crossed the Turkish border through the same narrow gap beneath the spikes.

I met this shirt for the first time when a hot young guy was putting his arms through the sleeves. This was in the barrany of Hammam Al-Jdid in Bab Sarija, a few months before the protests broke out in Damascus. This man was in the prime of life with a thick beard and cheerful smile. He was putting on his clothes and it seemed he had just finished in the hammam, while I was taking off my clothes ready to go in. He came so close to me that I could see water dripping from his beard, and he smelled of soap. He was wearing a shirt but his buttons were still undone, showing his hairy chest and belly, and he had wrapped a wet beige towel around his waist. He reached out a hand in greeting and introduced himself as Sebastián from Spain, a tourist on his last night in Damascus. Automatically, I put back on the clothes I had taken off and invited him to dinner in my house in the old city. He said yes.

I left him waiting by the fountain in the courtyard with a glass of ice water while I prepared dinner.

From the kitchen window overlooking the courtyard, I could see him examining the window arches, the ornate wooden arcades, and the stained glass in the windows. He took pictures of every detail in the courtyard: the stairs that led to the roof with a pot of basil on each step, the branches and blossoms of jasmine which reached over the balustrade, the lemon tree in the centre of the courtyard by the fountain, the autumn lemons that had dropped into its water. I called him from the kitchen and asked if he liked my house. He said he felt as though he was in his own city of Córdoba. He felt at home.

I prepared lamb meatballs with sour cherry sauce, a dish never missing from my fridge. I made up two plates and filled two glasses with local arak. He said everything on the table was new to him; he loved the meatballs and sour cherry sauce but couldn't stand the arak because it was too strong. I told him I had felt the same burning sensation when I tried it for the first time—it took a little while to get used to.

Sebastián preferred beer to arak, and fortunately I had two bottles of Syrian Barada in my fridge. He said he had drunk Barada before in one of the bars in the medina and he liked its strong wheaty flavour. He was hoping to take some back to Spain with him.

Not even the whole length of dinner gave me enough time to gaze at him. He was at his sexiest when summoning up enough English to make himself understood. He was so alluring, sitting in my courtyard, surrounded by my plants with the jasmine trellis behind him, eating my favourite dish. I told him of my dream of working in politics and advocating for gay rights in Syria, but when he yawned twice, I changed the topic to the hammams.

When darkness fell and the temperature didn't, Sebastián asked if he could take off his shirt. I said, "Please do." I didn't turn on the lamps in the courtyard because the lights of the city illuminating the sky were enough for us, along with the faint glow from a couple of candles floating on the surface of the water in the fountain.

As Sebastián took off his shirt, his arm hit the container with the sour cherry sauce. It spilled onto his shirt. Aghast, I immediately blamed myself. I leapt up at once and rushed around the table to help him take it all the way off. When I asked if I could wash it for him, he took it from my hand and dropped it on the ground. He took my arm, pulled it roughly towards him, and wrapped it around his bare waist.

Sebastián left the following day, having borrowed a clean shirt from my wardrobe. He sent me a text from the airport, saying he was wearing the shirt he had taken from me for his return journey to Spain, and he wanted me to keep his as a souvenir of that warm night.

Two years later, when I decided to leave Syria, I couldn't think of anything to wear for the journey that would be softer or more comfortable than this shirt. It felt like the embrace of its owner. That year, when I learned the Barada brewery in Qudsaya had been burned to the ground, the first person I thought of was Sebastián.

Aleppo, Winter 2012

These I bought from a renowned Armenian shoe-maker on my last trip to Aleppo. It had been my late mother's favourite shop. She always used to take me with her when I was a child, and every time she visited Aleppo, she would buy shoes for herself and her friends Um Elias and Um Saleh. My mother would believe anything this Armenian shoemaker told her. If he said these particular shoes were without doubt the most comfortable and the last of their kind in the shop, she would believe him and buy them without hesitation. He made shoes for women and men but never for children. Now that I was grown up, I decided to visit his shop myself so I could finally have my very own pair crafted by this Armenian master. On that last visit, his hair had turned completely grey, and he had started wearing round spectacles that rested on the very tip of his nose. When I mentioned my mother, he remembered her with a smile and a prayer. The shop seemed much smaller than in my memories and was brimming with pairs of shoes which left only a narrow space for him, his machine, and his workbench. The table was covered with pictures of the Holy Virgin embracing the messiah and pictures of Christian saints. When I asked him if he had any shoes in size forty-two, he smiled and replied he had the last pair in that size, the best of the shoes he had made recently. Without moving from his spot, he picked up a black plastic bag from the shelf and tossed it towards me. I caught it and opened it. Inside I found a pair of boots made of honey-brown leather. The colour was vile but I had no choice—I had to do just what my mother used to. I believed they were the best and the last pair he had made, and I bought them at once. In truth, despite the colour, I respected the craftsmanship that had gone into making them: the robust stitching, the strong soles, the careful cut of the leather. I didn't wear them much but I looked after them as if they had a soul. I kept them in the bottom of my wardrobe in a cloth bag, and occasionally I would take them out just to study the exquisite stitching and durability of the leather.

Their sturdiness was a prophecy. I hadn't known back then I would need those thick soles during my journey on foot. And they really were kind to my feet the whole way. They trod on pebbles and sank into mud and carried me from country to country. They kept me alive. I always used to say if these boots could talk, they would be the most truthful narrator of my story. And here they are today, in my hand— worn-out, open-mouthed like hungry beasts, begging to be allowed to stay.

The Leopard-Print Jockstrap

Istanbul, 2014

The smallest items of clothing have the longest stories. This was a pouch of soft, smooth, leopard-print fabric, surrounded by straps of black leather that made the bare buttocks stand out seductively. It was the first jockstrap that ever wore me.

I never imagined I would undertake a treacherous journey on a rubber dinghy while wearing a jockstrap under my clothes, as if I was on my way to an orgy or a dark room in some small European bar. In the middle of the sea between Turkey and Greece, more than forty people—men, women, children, and teenagers—were all calling out the Takbir and reciting chapters from the Qur'an as loudly as they could. I squeezed my backside, naked beneath my thin trousers. *Oh God, if this boat sinks and my body washes ashore and they send it to my brothers in Syria, my whole family will see I made this journey with my ass hanging out like I died in a strip club. They'd be so embarrassed ... there'd be such a scandal.* The prayer filled the space like an Islamic chorus in a mosque. Images of my rotting body, flung onto the Mediterranean shore still wearing the leopard-print jockstrap, flitted through my mind. Terror made me join in the chorus, and I repeated after them, "God is the greatest and praise be to Him, glory be to Him who subjects us to this, and we are not His equals." I was soon one of the loudest and most fervent worshippers. The woman squatting next to me began to recite the Qur'an over my head and blow on my face, urging me to calm down. We reached the shore of Greece safe and sound, although we all had to jump into the cold water which came up to our waists to reach the land.

We could now be called *survivors*. The survivors began to cry with joy and hug each other, even women and men who had never met before—despite being strangers, the force of their joy could only be discharged through an embrace. The woman who had been squatting next to me praised my deep faith, my prayers, and my piety throughout the journey—she was certain they were the reason for the boat's survival. I wished I could take off my soaking trousers and show them all the real reason I had been so afraid.

I arrived in Istanbul to join a caravan of Waiting Syrians. That's the name I gave them: The Waiting. We were all waiting for something, anything, to happen, whether it was the end of the war and a return to Syria, or a call from some business owner either accepting or refusing a request for work, or (more often) a call from a smuggler to take us to one of the beaches in Turkey so we could cross to Europe. Istanbul wasn't ideal for gay refugees like me. A gay Syrian refugee lives in danger in Istanbul, much like the Turkish gay man himself. Still, Istanbul wasn't a normal city—it was like a sea witch, entangling everyone who visited in her hair and intoxicating them with the scent of the ocean. The city sorceress wrapped me in her damp hair, made me drunk on her perfume and invited me to recline on her shoulder. I wasn't confined to my bed in the hostel, waiting for a call from the smuggler like all the other Waiting. Exactly the opposite—the smell of coffee led me to the lanes of Beyoğlu. Istanbul's long summer nights were like a cloud over my head, raining only on me, washing away a little more of my sadness each night. I had no fear of nights in Istanbul despite their reputation. Each evening I went to bars heaving with Turks and tourists and ended up in the gay club Tekyon. It was the most appropriate cellar for the Waiting Gays, offering everything that might ease the burden of what we had been through: alcohol, dancing, music, fumbling and rubbing against each other, sex with strangers. Every night in Istanbul was like my last.

My final night in Tekyon, I was standing in my favourite nook under the stripper's stage when a red spotlight fell on my head. I was holding a bottle of beer, and my eyes were fixed in the direction of a very tall man in the other section. In the darkness, I couldn't see much more than the wolfish gleam in his eyes. But when the lights of the glitterball fell on him, I discovered, little by little, his brawny body and rock-hard forearms, his smooth chest peeping out through the open collar of his loose shirt. He too was holding a bottle of beer, and there was a black curtain behind him. In the darkness, he smiled at me. He raised his bottle to me, and I did the same in return. He walked right over to me until we were touching—he was so tall that the top of my head only reached his armpit. A delicious smell of sweat wafted off him. His smooth face had Latin features. He was incredibly sexy. He introduced himself as Noah from America and I replied, "I'm Furat." He said, "Are you from Iraq?" I started to explain my name in ornamented English, "I'm from Syria. The Furat, known in English as the Euphrates, passes through Syria before crossing Iraq. It crosses three governorates: Northern Aleppo, Raqqa, and Deir Ezzor. The most well-known Syrian city located on the banks of the Euphrates is Deir Ezzor, because of its famous suspension bridge and its oilfields." He burst out laughing; there was a deep dimple in his cheek, and he had dazzling white teeth. He wrapped his solid arm around my neck and hugged me close. My right ear was pressed against his chest. He said, "Ya'ny, you didn't realise that I speak Arabic better than you ... How come you speak English?" he said in Arabic, in an accent that was pure Iraqi.

Noah had spent seven years in Baghdad after the Americans invaded Iraq in 2003 and he learnt Arabic there through his humanitarian work. After the US withdrew, he moved to Istanbul to work on projects supporting the Syrian resistance. I didn't tell him I was a journalist so I wouldn't have to dive into a political discussion I didn't want to have. Instead, I started to talk about Madonna and Britney Spears, shouting over the loud music. He refilled my glass whenever it was empty and called for shots more than once. I had never drunk so much in my life, but I couldn't refuse a single drink from his honeyed voice filled with words that stroked and teased me like feathers.

I let his hands play with my body among the crowd of men. He dragged me onto the dancefloor, and we became one body swaying to a song of Hande Yener's that was a hit in 2014—I remember the chorus went *Ya ya ya ya*. Waterfalls of blue and red light poured onto our heads, and I stared at his gorgeous lips as he sang along perfectly to the Turkish words. His lips entranced me. "Let's go back to mine," he whispered into my ear in Arabic.

We headed to the cloakroom and picked up a black leather gym bag and jacket. He put on the jacket, stuck his hand in his pocket, and said nonchalantly in Arabic, "Oh no, not again—my apartment keys have fallen out of my pocket."

The women of Syria have a saying to laugh at men: "When a man's got an erection, his brain stops working, and *that's* the moment to take advantage of him." And so, it took no effort on Noah's part to convince me to go with him to the hotel next to the nightclub.

He pulled me by the hand like a lamb to the slaughter. We went into the hotel, nondescript other than the turquoise velvet sofa in the lobby that I lay down on while he spoke to the receptionist in English: "A room for two for the night, please." And he paid in cash. He took my hand and led me to the elevator, and as soon as it stopped on the third floor, he picked me up in his powerful arms, my head dangling over his forearm so the corridor was upside-down. We went into the room, and he threw me onto the bed. My limp body sank into the soft whiteness. I closed my eyes and decided to enjoy myself.

He started to kiss every inch of my body and he pulled at my clothes until he had me completely naked. Then he stood up, opened his black bag, and took out some black leather straps, some sex toys, and a jockstrap. He trod on my neck with his heavy boots and dressed me in the jockstrap, and he began kissing my bare cheeks, lapping away with his slippery tongue. I felt as though I were flying, and my blood was tickling my veins. He bound my wrists behind me with leather and chains and dipped his tongue in my anus as though he were tasting cream.

The sound of my ringtone tore through this scene and my phone screen blinked inside the pocket of the trousers tossed on the floor. Noah threw his heavy body on top of me and sighed with all his might into my ear, as if he wanted to shut off my hearing and my sight. The phone wouldn't stop ringing. I fluttered beneath him like a wounded bird—I couldn't catch my breath. The sound of the mobile got louder and louder. He got up, freed my hands, and told me to turn my phone off. When I picked up the phone I found eleven missed calls from the smuggler. Noah brought his face close to mine to kiss me, and I smacked him away. I tried to get up off the bed but I fell onto the floor and my cheek crashed into my honey-brown boots—it was only at that moment I noticed how old and cracked they looked. I hadn't realised Noah had bound my ankles with a leather strap. I scrambled to free my feet, snatched up my red-checked shirt and my trousers from the ground, and pulled them on in a panic. I picked up my boots and raced out of the room. The receptionist gave me a smile and said something in Turkish while I sat on the turquoise sofa, pulled on my boots, and tied the laces tight. I left the hotel and threw myself into the first taxi I saw. "Aksaray, please."

The taxi stopped in front of the hostel and I found my roommates waiting for me on the pavement with the smuggler Ali Baba (who got his name by claiming that he would never smuggle more than forty people at a time on a dinghy).

"Lucky you got here in time. Go get your papers from the safe and get back here, the bus is leaving in two minutes," said Ali Baba.

The Red Hoodie

Åseda, July 2014

A jacket to protect me from the cold of summer. This is an exotic concept for Syrians, one that will only make sense to those recently arrived in Sweden. The red hoodie was the first piece of clothing I bought in Sweden. It was from H&M in Växjö, the only place I could enter with confidence and buy something new due to the meagre allowance from the Immigration Bureau. I love this hoodie, which I have clung to since my first month in Sweden. In one of the pockets I kept the letter from the Immigration Bureau, the one refusing to buy the jacket. On the back of it I noted down a story.

During one of the regular tea-drinking sessions with my roommates in the asylboende in Åseda, one of them posed a question to all of us: Why did you choose Sweden as your country of refuge? The first said he wanted his children to have the safest future, but in reality he was the one who had reached safety and he had left his kids in Aleppo—he didn't know when he would get a residence permit and be able to reunite his family. Another said he wanted to complete his studies in civil engineering and find a well-paid job. A third said he was exhausted after three years of fleeing from bombing and he decided to come to rest in these forests. He said he wanted to become a farmer in Sweden. Another said he had reached Sweden so he could have a house, a fridge filled with food, fruit and vegetables, and clean water, even if he had to live at the northernmost point of the country. Yet another said he wanted to obtain Swedish citizenship so he could spread his wings and fly wherever he could find work without the burden of a visa. The youngest was in his early twenties. He said he wanted to enjoy freedom of every kind in this country. He wanted to go to the mosque for prayers and meditation without being subjected to security questioning, to go to a nudist beach, drink alcohol, have sex with his girlfriend, all without being judged by society for his contradictions. One interrupted to say he was running away from his wife who wouldn't shut up, and now he was relieved to be living among men without any gossiping, nagging women—and, he said, he had learned about artificial cunts, the best thing that had happened to him in Sweden. The rest of the men burst out laughing and raised their cups of tea to him, toasting their arrival in a land of safety. Then one of them said, "Furat, your turn—why did you choose Sweden?"

Nietzsche says, "Silence is worse; all truths that are kept silent become poisonous."

I turned over the letter. That day I chose silence and excused myself to go to my room. And as usual I wrote down everything I wanted to tell them but couldn't say out loud.

I escaped the same war you all did. I escaped the same sword that would have sliced your necks, the barrel bombs that could crush your flesh and bones with the stones of your own homes. I escaped with only a small rucksack, leaving behind my home, my family, my work, my loved ones, my memories. Just like you. We gave up our lives and whatever money we were able to bring out of Syria to the criminal smugglers so they could throw us into the same death boats. We walked for miles over the same rough stones and rail tracks, more afraid of what awaited us than of what we were leaving behind. I love you all and believe we are all brothers in war. I shared a homeland with you, I shared the horrors of war, and I stand beside you as you yearn for freedom. And today I share exile with you. I am part of your present and future. Today, having reached safety, we all sat together and shared the reasons we had for choosing Sweden as our adopted country. I envy you. All of you have absolute freedom to respond to this question—all except me.

I came here to be accepted, not tolerated. To live in a society that respects me for who I am and does not judge me for what I do in the privacy of my bedroom. My wish is very simple: not a large apartment for my kids, or a place at university, or even a well-paid job. I came here looking for love. I don't ask you to celebrate my being gay. All I want is respect for who I am—the same respect I earned from you for helping you translate your letters. Even if you aren't gay yourself, remember that your children might be. Choose to love them. Remember this and remember me.

I decided to drop the letter in our apartment's letterbox before leaving the asylboende.

I left the letter for the asylum seekers who would come after us. More than a million were crossing the Mediterranean. And not just the letter—I left the jackets, jumpers, and snow boots I bought from the second-hand shops, all folded neatly and placed in the wardrobe, awaiting their arrival.

I left quietly, like a housecat grown bored of warmth and hankering after some adventure in the outside world. I left the asylboende in the same clothes I wore to leave Syria, but to that outfit I added the red hoodie and my mother's wisdom:

"Nothing stays the same, everything changes eventually. Look at your little feet—they won't stay that size forever! And not just your shoe size. Everything changes, yabny, and nothing stays as it is. The day we are living right now will be in the past by tomorrow. So don't be sad if we have some rough times. You can be sure one day it will all be in the past."

CHAPTER 10

Tattoo

The last time I studied a foreign language was in the summer of 2011 in Syria. The Centre Culturel Français—the CCF—in Damascus offered free courses to journalists and those in the cultural sector. I was diligent in going to the centre every day; it became my second home. It was a contemporary building, designed by the French architect José Oubrebrie in the mid-eighties. Its modern, slightly Western design stood out in the Sarouja neighbourhood, one of the most beautiful parts of Damascus, where the housefronts were constructed from stone with beechwood columns emerging above. It was always tempting to linger in the neighbourhood once French lessons were done. Wherever you went, the songs of Um Kulthoum and Fairuz could be heard, each competing to outdo the other. On the side streets, the laughter of young men and women rang out constantly, their eyes glinting as they flirted. There were girls whose heads were covered with white hijabs, and others who wore clothes showing their shoulders. The beautiful, beautiful, beautiful girls of Damascus. So much passionate adoration, so much rapturous desire could be found there.

My friends and I reached with eager hands for sha-warma sandwiches and bowls of fuul, catching them gently from the waiters' fingertips as they swooped overhead. My favourite dish was fried egg with hou-mous drenched in Syrian olive oil, surrounded by pickled cucumber and all kinds of fresh vegetables. Shisha pipes passed among us with smouldering coals on top because why would we sit there without a cloud of fragrant smoke? A summer breeze would blow on the coals so the space was filled with sparks like fireworks. Time spent in Sarouja was always a celebration.

The Arab Spring arrived in Sarouja, and the side streets were filled with young revolutionaries. The cafés became covert minbars for defiant speeches and the setting-off point for flash protests against the regime. The protestors would head to the alleyways of the medina and hold up placards with slogans de-manding change, then they would take photographs and send them to the news channels. If the protests went on for any longer than a few minutes, the protes-tors would wind up in prison or murdered by security forces who were scattered all throughout the streets. Security services were spread thickly around Sarouja, and anyone passing through the area became an object of suspicion and might well be arrested. Just sitting in a café in Sarouja became an arrestable charge. So I went there only for my French classes, and if I had time I would go to bathe and relax in Hammam Al-Khanji to meet older men in secret. No one went there anymore apart from the locals and the market traders because of the security checkpoints between Damascus and the surrounding countryside.

My last visit to the CCF was in July 2011 when I went to pick up the results of a French exam I had taken. I found the iron gates of the centre closed and locked. The names of the students appeared behind the iron bars like prisoners. I realised the French had closed the centre and stopped their activities because of the worsening situation. On the same day I had an appointment with my friend, a tattooist, at his house—he was afraid of tattooing my back and neck in his studio because, he said, the design I had emailed was itself a capital offence.

His tattoo needle punctured my back as he began to carve out a crescent. At first it felt like the needle was splitting my back in two, but before long the pain transformed into a pleasant tickle. I wanted the flag of Tunisia, where the Arab Spring began, on the back of my neck, but the tattooist cheated and placed it on my upper back. "It's a death warrant in this country, they'll have your head," he said. I never did display it in Damascus, taking care to hide it beneath my collar. I only showed my tattoo openly in Hammam Al-Khanji and in the mirror in my house.

There I was today, in the bathroom of my house in Gothenburg, turning my back to the mirror, scrutinising the crescent moon and star tattooed there. I took the towel hanging behind the door, dried my body, and wrapped it around my waist. I brought my face close to the mirror and examined my cheeks to see if there were any hairs I needed to pluck, but couldn't find any. I picked up the hairdryer, dried my thick black beard so it looked smoother and went to my room where I pulled on a T-shirt with a wide neck; I didn't care whether or not it showed my tattoo. I finished getting dressed, sprayed some Davidoff Blue on my neck and wrists, picked up my canvas bag with *Freedom* printed on it in Arabic, and left to catch Tram 11 heading from Saltholmen to Majorna. It was my first day of class at SFI—Swedish for Immigrants.

SFI

It wasn't hard to find the school building in Majorna. All I had to do was walk behind a gaggle of young people. They had got off at the same stop as me, but their tram had come from the opposite direction. Before I heard them say a word, I knew they were Syrian from their smart haircuts, their eyebrows like swords, their thick eyelashes; their meticulously styled beards, their immaculate, carefully ironed clothes, and their gleaming shoes. They were walking like a dabke troupe, jumping around each other and waving their arms in the air to make their point.

I walked behind them into the spacious garden of a large red-brick building that reminded me of the Capuchin Church in Deir Ezzor.

I pushed the heavy wooden door open with both hands and went inside. The smell took me back to the moment I entered the asylboende for the first time, the same fragrance of Eastern, Asian, and African spices, but this time mixed with the aroma of Swedish coffee. I climbed the stairs to the first floor, walked along several corridors, then came more stairs. Migrants of every colour were distributed along the corridors. The classroom doors were open, revealing huddles of women in the corners. Announcement boards filled the walls: the Språk Café language exchange, Arabic music concerts, a play about refugees, posters advertising the Red Cross. I noticed small rainbow flags on the teachers' tables and the information windows—those flags were silent smiles at me. I kept walking and climbing until I found the classroom with the same number the teacher had texted me. I paused in the doorway of a large classroom filled with students chatting before the teacher arrived.

Keeping my eyes on the ground, I walked to the very last chair and sat down. The only words I knew in Swedish were *Hej* and *Hej da*—hello and goodbye. I tried to take a deep breath and failed. I tried again and felt suffocated. The hall was painted a depressing shade of beige. Coat pegs were fixed on the wall. A whiteboard had some phrases written on it, apparently left over from the previous class. A large, tall window let in the light. I furtively peeked at the faces of the other students and at first all of them were talking, totally oblivious to me, like I was a ghost. I opened my bag, took out my blue notebook, and placed it in front of me. Then I took out my pencil and laid it on top of the notebook. I took a deep breath and looked again at the other students, more carefully this time. There was a group of women in hijabs all swathed in black like widows in mourning; they looked to be middle-aged. They appeared to know each other well, one of them even putting her hand around the shoulders of another while they were talking. Arab men of different ages were sitting around in groups, each separate from the other.

Clearly, each group was discussing different topics. The youngest group, with three men, was absorbed in scribbling on some printed sheets. There was a woman whose age I couldn't guess because I couldn't see her face—it was covered by a round mass of curly hair. She was sitting by herself, immersed in writing in her notebook. She had put lots of colourful plastic bracelets and accessories on her arms and she was wearing short pink fishnet gloves that showed her gleaming pink nails. Directly behind her, and also sitting alone, was a golden-skinned girl who looked like the girls from the countryside in northern Syria. Her nose was hooked, and her soft black hair hung over her shoulders.

I opened the notebook to write the date like I used to do in primary school, and while I was writing I picked out some phrases from the conversations around me. "How lovely ... he has great halal meat ... come on, man, she's too old ... I got a new letter ... my kid's school ... Yousef loves them fried ... his veils are so pretty you'll lose your mind ... family reunion ... poor thing can't find anywhere to rent." These words were interrupted by the sound of stiletto heels tapping on the classroom floor. I raised my head and faced a woman with her features painted on with makeup. Tattooed eyebrows, long, black eyelashes, and dark eyes. She had coloured her thick lips crimson. On her head she wore a hijab made of shiny cheetah-print satin. The ends of her scarf were hidden inside the collar of her tight-fitting blouse whose buttons seemed on the verge of popping open. The sleeves of her blouse were see-through, showing off her plump white arms. Her stout waist was clasped by a thick belt of gold-plated chains, woven through a huge gold padlock that hung over her crotch. She wore tight black trousers over her full thighs, and she carried a large golden handbag with several outer pockets and metal locks. Everything she wore was tight, so that her body appeared like a ticking bomb about to explode. In honour of her animal-print hijab, I called her Tiger Woman.

Tiger Woman swooped in on the group of women in hijabs, crying "Salaam aleikum" in a loud condescending tone. Some of them responded, others paid her no attention. She sat down among them and put her golden handbag on her thighs, but after less than a minute she thrust her hand into the bag reaching for her mobile phone. She stood up and left the classroom, then returned a few seconds later, her bottom lip in her mouth. This time, she sat in the front row away from the other women. She crossed her arms on the desk in front of her and buried her head in them.

Suddenly everyone stopped talking. The groups of young students scattered, just as the protestors in Syria used to flee when security forces arrived. The students moved apart and looked ahead at the board.

A tall woman entered wearing a loose black dress that covered her knees—it looked like a cloth bag with long sleeves. She had tied back her curly blonde hair with a long black ribbon. She dragged a red plastic trolley basket behind her like the ones I had seen in the supermarket, but this one was full of books and sheets of paper. I guessed she was the teacher. She parked the trolley behind her, looked at us with a broad smile and said, "Hej!" She seemed to be in her late thirties. Tiger Woman ignored her and didn't move, and the teacher didn't look at or address her at all. The teacher singled me out with a glance and a smile, apparently welcoming me as a new student. I returned her smile. Tiger Woman shifted her head and sat up a little. She was trying to peek at her phone, placed on her plump thighs.

The teacher said something in Swedish I didn't understand, interrupted by the sound of the curly-haired woman's accessories clanking together as she stood up to arrange her clothes and ran her fingers through her thick hair, briefly revealing a wrinkled face. She had Mediterranean features and spoke in accented English, "Let's introduce ourselves to the new students." She nodded towards the teacher and went on, "They usually don't understand any Swedish." Then she sat down again. I wanted to thank her, but another student began to introduce himself in Swedish, and after two more students it was my turn. Staring at Tiger Woman I said, "Je m'appelle Furat, je suis syrien."

The teacher's face wasn't the only one that showed confusion. Most students turned to me with enquiring looks on their faces. Even Tiger Woman briefly raised her head, but it soon dropped back into its den. That moment took me back to my days in primary school in Deir Ezzor, when I would recite French texts with prodigious care, and the others would crack jokes that my mother tongue was French because my mother was a French teacher at the school. The teacher smiled at me a second time then took a pen from the trolley, turned her back to us and went to the whiteboard. Although her dress had a high collar, I noticed the tip of a tattoo at the bottom of her neck, in the same place where I had one. While

I was staring at the teacher's neck and tracing different shapes of her tattoo in my imagination, the body of one of the young guys blocked it from view when he stood up and sat down next to the curly-haired woman. Then he turned to the other young guys and winked at them.

The teacher drew a human head on the board. A head without features. Then she bent over so she was plunged into the trolley. When she stood up, her face was the colour of beetroot and she was holding a sheaf of paper. She put a paper on the first desk next to Tiger Woman's head, then walked quickly between the seats, tossing a paper in front of each student. She was like the beggars on the buses in Syria when they hurriedly throw a chapter of the Qur'an into the laps of the passengers to force them to pay up. She continued this process until she reached me. She smiled at me a third time and handed me a paper. I exchanged another smile with her then looked at the paper to find a human head in my hands, of unknown age and gender. It opened large eyes and gazed at me with a vacant smile. The teacher finished handing out the heads and threw the ones that were left into her trolley. Every student had a human head. The classroom was crammed with heads: our heads, the heads in our hands, the teacher's head, the head on the board, the heads in the teacher's trolley. I felt suffocated and I stood up to open the window before resuming my seat.

The teacher began to draw features on the head, saying the words in Swedish. Tiger Woman moved her head again. The teacher carried on speaking, then asked the students to take turns reading. I tried to decipher the symbols around the head. "Furat," the teacher called on me. It was my turn. The page was completely blank. The head disappeared and the words around it fled. A thin black hand came from behind me and reached towards my paper. Like a magic wand, it returned the head to the page. The hand pointed at a word: *mun*. Before I could read it, the voices of the other students sounded out together: *mun mun mun mun*. I recited it as the voices urged, then I raised my head in the teacher's direction. She smiled at me again. I looked at Tiger Woman but she wasn't there; she wasn't in the classroom at all. The teacher said something in Swedish I didn't understand, but the other students were apparently preparing to go out of the classroom, leaving their books behind. The young guys left the classroom immediately. The women in hijabs took plastic bags and lunchboxes out of their handbags. As for the wheat-skinned countryside girl, she too had buried her head as if surrendering to sleep. The same hand that had reached out earlier was now extended to me in greeting.

It belonged to a skinny young Black guy with a handsome face and sweet smile. He carried a lunchbox. He introduced himself in French and invited me to have lunch with him in the basement canteen, but as it was a sunny day I said I'd rather go outside. He said he wanted to be my friend. He pressed his warm palm against my sweaty one. He withdrew his hand reluctantly and walked to the door, glancing back at me with a smile.

In the courtyard the students were engaged in a smoking marathon while they had the opportunity. I found my young classmates standing in a corner holding steaming paper cups and smoking. I joined them and said, "Marhaba." A few of them replied, "Ahlan." One of them offered me a cigarette, which I refused. Another was talking in a thick Aleppo accent about the room he was renting for a thousand kronor a month, apparently some kind of wardrobe—he described it as a grave. Another man headed over to me and said, in a Damascus accent, "What did you do for work in Syria?" I told him I was a journalist. "Aouz bi-Allah," he said, disgust visible on his face. A second guy turned to him; he too had a Damascus accent. "Are you OK, ya zalma, he said he's a journalist, not that he's gay." The first one replied, "Nothing ruined Syria more than journalists." Then he said sourly, "I'm joking of course ... Don't take it so seriously."

Yet another place in this country where I had to hide my identity, when I had once believed all my secrets would slide off my shoulders the instant I left the asylboende. These guys in their early twenties— what did they know about being gay in Syria? By the time they became adults the war had already begun. Their only references for what it's like being gay were the comedies that Syrian and Arab TV channels showed during the Arab Spring, and which were often shared on social media, all of them deriding gay men. Or, if it was a TV drama, the gay man would be a sinner, a source of shame to his family and to society. The concept of freedom was distorted to these young people; when gay people demanded their rights it was a perversion of the morals and customs of religion and society.

The same student from Damascus carried on talking, this time about the teacher, saying that she wasn't very attractive. A third student said to me in an Iraqi accent, "Are you Iraqi or Syrian?" I told him I was from Deir Ezzor. He nodded, indicating his familiarity with my accent, which was very similar to the accent found in western Iraq. "The Syrian girl isn't very sexy either, she walks like a man." "The old lady in class with us is much prettier." "But the Swedish girls are so hot, ya zalma." "Wallahi, every single one that rides the tram with me … gorgeous." "Where can I meet these girls, I only meet ancient ones … Even the Arab ladies in class are my mother's age."

Sex dominated the conversation. I felt like I was with a bunch of teenagers in high school, where women were the main topic of conversation. But what I found interesting about these straight men was their discussion of how to treat Swedish girls in public. They said Swedish girls weren't comfortable if you got close to them or touched them in the tram; they would only look at a guy with Middle Eastern features if he avoided getting close, as if they assumed he must be a chauvinist or a fundamentalist.

Suddenly the curly-haired woman was standing among us. "The horny lady's arrived," whispered the Iraqi. The curly-haired woman spoke to one of the students in a western Syrian accent; he took a packet of cigarettes out of his pocket and handed her one. She took it from him, turned to me, and said, "What brought you to Sweden?" But before I could reply she had moved towards the most handsome of the boys and brought her cigarette up to her face, an indication that he should light it, which he did at once.

"Hey man, it seems like she already knows you," said the student from Damascus. The boys began winking and teasing her. "Be careful she doesn't fall for you." The curly-haired woman excused herself, saying, "I'm going to the bathroom ... Does anyone want to join me?" Raucous laughter followed her as she went in, leaving behind a cloud of smoke. They told me she was married to a Syrian man who lived in the Gulf and was cruel to her, and she had escaped him and fled to Turkey. From there she took a boat, like all the other refugees who arrived here.

All of a sudden I felt a warm hand on my neck. "Nice tattoo." I turned around and saw a huge golden crucifix surrounded by glorious chest hair. My gaze travelled up the chunky gold chain until it reached the face of a huge man. I had already noticed him in the classroom—although his beard was full, he couldn't be more than twenty. I found this bear incredibly sexy. I pulled my T-shirt down further to show him the whole tattoo and, borrowing a Syrian phrase, I said, "If you want it, it's yours." A smile flooded his face and he said, "Thanks, habibi." "Breaktime's over," the Aleppan student said. I climbed the stairs, sticking close to the Sexy Bear. Even though I was making it hard for him to walk, he didn't move away from me—on the contrary, he rubbed against me, even putting his arm around my neck as you might do to a friend. When we reached the classroom door, he excused himself and went to the bathroom.

I re-entered the classroom. Tiger Woman was in her seat. There was rage on her face, and her long crimson nails tapped furiously on her phone screen as though replying to ten messages at once. The Black guy had moved and was sitting in my seat. I sat next to him and said in French, "Nice to meet you." He put his hand on my thigh and squeezed it with a smile. We were startled by the sound of Tiger Woman's phone slamming onto the floor. She said, "Fuck those fucking cunts." She stood up and bent towards us, lifting her round ass towards the door to pick her phone off the floor. Just then, Aleppan Student came in the classroom—when he saw Tiger Woman in this position he froze. From where I was sitting it looked exactly as though he was fucking her ass. The Black student and I looked at each other; he smiled and winked. He moved his hand a little further up my thigh. Tiger Woman and Aleppan Student sat back down.

The women in hijabs came in, their handbags smelling of coriander and garlic. They seemed excited and were discussing food. "Thank you for your assistance, Lord." "I'm used to cooking over a fire ... I don't like that all the ovens here are electric." "I don't know where Yousef got the lamb." "Ya ikhti, after the meat in Syria, there's nothing else. Talk about fresh ... The butcher used to slaughter a sheep every day."

Tiger Woman had gone out as soon as the women in hijabs came in. When she came back in, her phone was in her hand. She went out again and came back in, her phone in her hand. She grumbled under her breath and buried her head in her arms once more.

The young guys entered the classroom with the curly-haired woman. They sat together, the woman in the middle. The golden-skinned girl came in with her hair covering her face and sat in her isolated seat. Sexy Bear came in and took a seat next to mine, putting his large hand on my neck. I was now sitting between Black Guy and Sexy Bear.

The teacher came in carrying a naked and headless human body. She closed the classroom door behind her and lay the body flat on the table, then turned her back to us and wrote *kroppen* on the blackboard. The smell of cooking still filled the air. Black Guy was still clutching my thigh. The teacher picked up the body and leaned it against the board. The smell of cooking got stronger. Sexy Bear had forgotten to zip up his trousers, and the gap widened, showing his loose, water-spotted underwear. Black Guy squeezed my leg as hard as he could.

My phone went off—the ringtone was a Dalida song.

Je ne rêve plus je ne fume plus

Je n'ai même plus d'histoire

I opened the bag to silence my phone but Black Guy grabbed my hand. "Leave it. It's the most beautiful thing here." Without letting go, he pulled my hand and placed it on his skinny thigh.

Je suis sale sans toi

Je suis laide sans toi

He took my pencil and softly ran it over my neck. He put his hand on my neck and pulled me towards him until my lips touched his. The teacher underlined the word *kroppen* on the board. Black Guy ran his warm tongue over my lower lip, took my hand from his thigh, and put it on his erect penis. I started rubbing it for him, and he rubbed mine until I was hard as well.

Je suis comme un orphelin dans un dortoir

Curly-Haired Woman had unzipped all the young men's trousers and pulled out their dicks, and now she sat beneath her seat and began sucking them. I felt something warm and wet fall on the back of my neck. Sexy Bear spat on my tattoo then lapped up his own spit. The scent of cooking filled the air.

Je n'ai plus envie de vivre ma vie

The body of a freshly skinned lamb hung over the head of each woman, and blood was dripping onto their heads from the lambs' necks. The women gathered in a ring around a large black pot that was bubbling over a fire. Thick steam rose and filled the air. Golden-Skinned Girl stood on the edge of the pot, covering her face with her soft, smooth hair.

Je n'ai plus de vie, et même mon lit

Tiger Woman was video-calling a man whose red tongue filled the screen of her mobile as he passed it over his bushy moustache. She had taken off her pants and now she began to lick and spit on her red nails before she rubbed them against the edge of her pussy. Moans and grunts could be heard in every direction. Curly-Haired Woman's cheeks inflated as she swallowed two cocks at the same time. She opened her shirt so her breasts were bare. Iraqi Man rode on my chest like he was mounting a horse; he put his dick in my mouth as he sucked Tiger Woman's nipples. I closed my eyes so I wouldn't see her pussy, which was almost swallowing my head. Iraqi Man took his cock out of my mouth and screamed, *"Nitshih! Fuck him!"* The teacher turned towards us and shouted at the top of her voice, "Kroppen." The young men were rubbing their nipples as they watched Curly-Haired Woman choking on cocks. Others were rubbing their dicks and spitting on her while they waited for their turn. The man's tongue came out of Tiger Woman's screen and began licking her pussy. Sexy Bear was asleep on the ground, and I fell off the chair on top of him. I fell asleep on his sweaty chest while the heads the teacher had handed out were scattered all over us. Black Guy was licking my ass. A collective moan shook the place. I was screaming from pleasure, and she was screaming from pleasure, and I could hear food boiling in the pot. The steam in the classroom condensed and everyone's features disappeared. Sexy Bear cried out in pain as I mercilessly clipped his chest hair.

Je verse mon sang dans ton corps

One of them pulled me off Sexy Bear and put me on my back so I could help Curly-Haired Woman suck the remaining students' dicks. My mouth turned into a pussy with a series of cocks sliding in and out. Iraqi Man began to play with Tiger Woman's breasts. He took them out of her bra and devoured them like a hungry baby. Black Guy tied my hands behind my back with his belt and threw me on the ground on top of the teacher's papers. Damascus Student put one heavy foot on top of my head and his other foot in my mouth. Black Guy grabbed my ass and opened it up for the Sexy Bear's hard cock. After Black Guy spat on my ring, Sexy Bear pushed his hard cock inside me all at once. I couldn't cry out or even catch a breath, because Damascus Student's foot filled my mouth. Black Guy lowered his head and started sucking my dick as if he was a calf suckling his mother's teat.

Et je suis comme un oiseau mort quand toi tu dors

Our groans filled the place. The teacher cut an arm off the human body and threw it at us, shouting, "Arm." Our moaning grew louder and louder and groans of pleasure overpowered the teacher's voice. Golden-Skinned Girl threw herself into the pot of boiling food, which sprayed our bodies and went all over the floor. The women took the bodies of the sheep that were attached to the ceiling and threw them in the pot so the girl's body disappeared in among them. Tiger Woman's call with the moustachioed man was cut off while Iraqi Man was ruthlessly riding her ass. The smell of boiling meat. Steam. Sexy Bear was asleep on top of me, crushing me with his huge body. Black Guy was sucking my cock from below as if he wanted to suck out my soul. Damascus Student stood and pissed on the three of us until we were soaked. The teacher cut a leg off the human body and threw it into the pot. "Leg." I screamed, "Arm," in reply and cut off the other arm. I tossed it and it landed between Tiger Woman's legs. The group of young men joined in and began to piss on us. The women kept stirring the food in the pot as if nothing was happening. Tiger Woman's phone wouldn't stop vibrating. The teacher shouted, "Knee." The man with the bushy moustache would not stop calling. Tiger Woman picked up her phone and pushed it into her pussy, and as it started to vibrate inside her, her screaming rose. The teacher shouted louder,

"Thigh." Damascus Student took his foot out of my mouth and replaced it with the foot of the leg that had been flung on the floor. The sound of groaning got louder. The teacher shouted, "Foot." Everyone was on the verge of orgasm. Sexy Bear was pushing his dick hard and fast inside me as if he wanted to push it out the other side. The teacher yelled, "Elbow."

Près de ma radio comme un gosse idiot
Écoutant sa propre voix qui chantera

The pace of thrusting and vibrating increased. The sound of moaning got louder and louder, Tiger Woman's voice dominating the others. The young men were rubbing their cocks faster and faster over the head of Curly-Haired Woman and she opened her mouth in anticipation. The teacher was chopping up human flesh and flinging it at us. The sound of penetration, panting, our bodies rubbing against each other, hoarse cries all rose together, and the women's bubbling cooking pot was loudest of all. Cum covered Curly-Haired Woman's face and her features disappeared as if she was a wax statue. Her tongue began to lick the stickiness beside her mouth. I filled Black Guy's mouth with my white milk, and he sprayed his over the heads spread out on the floor. Sexy Bear pulled his bloodied and shit-covered dick out of my asshole. He picked up a head from the ground and wiped his dick on it, then he spat on me. Tiger Woman was licking up the cum that Iraqi Man had sprayed on her breasts.

We all got dressed and collected the human heads that were stained with shit and piss and blood and food, and we put them in our bags. We gathered up the bits our teacher had cut off the human body and we put them on the torso stump, which we leaned against the blackboard next to the word *kroppen*. The women picked up the cooking pot that was brimming with food. We left the teacher dangling from the classroom ceiling; she had hung herself with her black hair ribbon. We left quietly and closed the door behind us.

Je suis malade
Complètement malade

CHAPTER 11

Selamlik 1

At midnight on June 6th, Liva Street in Cihangir stood in darkness. There was no entering this area without a struggle. The roadblocks set up by the protestors—barricades made of rubbish bins, wooden boxes, furniture, chairs, and sandbags—blocked movement in and out. I avoided running into the protestors as I walked, propelled equally by hope and fear. In my hand I carried a bottle of mineral water which I occasionally sprayed onto my face and rubbed into my eyes to counteract the effect of the tear gas. I wondered if this might be the last time I walked along these streets; perhaps, finally, my destiny would lead me to Europe. I stood in the middle of the sloping street. It was empty apart from me and an elderly dog who was staggering leisurely towards the end of the alley. I was meeting Baklawa so he could take me to Selamlik for the first time.

I had met him on my first night in Istanbul in a nightclub called Cheero. I heard him yelling in an Aleppan accent into the ear of another young guy on the dancefloor. After that we ran into each other at the bar, where he asked the barman to refill his white wine and put a beer for me on his tab, and conversation soon flowed. I liked the ease with which he carried himself, his strong personality, and his carnival clothes. I liked how he moved his arms in the air when speaking, as if expressing himself through dance, and the glitter eyeshadow he wore above the black kohl drawn Cleopatra-style over his bulging eyes. Most of all, I liked his boldness and utter lack of shame when he declared himself to be a sex worker in Istanbul. He expressed his intention of crossing to Europe as soon as he had enough money. That made me confess my own similar goal, and he immediately offered to take me to Selamlik.

I thought he was proposing to guide me around the famous palace selamlik in Istanbul, until he explained that he was talking about a brothel he worked in—it had been given the name Selamlik because, like the men's quarters in the palace, the brothel workers and clientele were all men. He wanted to introduce me to one of the "guaranteed" smugglers, as Baklawa described them, who in return for all the cash I had would help me to penetrate Europe's stronghold. When I asked Baklawa to take me there, he said, "Let's meet tomorrow," and raised a glass of wine with his fingertips, showing off the gold paint on his nails. "To your health. To the health of the Arab Spring, of Istanbul, of Europe."

The elderly dog began to bark as soon as we heard high heels on the pavement. A slim girl in a tight, one-shouldered black dress appeared from the darkness, flicking her long hair. She hurried towards me and hugged me into her spongy chest. I smelled perfume, something pleasant with a hint of sweets. It was Baklawa in his work clothes—I only recognised him by his goggle eyes and the distinctive way he wore his eyeliner. "Sorry for being late, I was visiting a client," he said as he planted red kisses on my cheeks. "It's never finished, wherever we go there's always problems," he said, referring to the protests and the police gatherings. He took my hand and led me inside a shadowy passageway that branched off from the street. "Mama Nabila is the owner of Selamlik—make sure you show her respect," he warned as we stopped in front of the entrance to a building where tissues, old plastic bags, and dog shit lay piled in heaps. It appeared to be uninhabited. I was alarmed by the sound of crashing cooking pots and metal implements, as if all the kitchens in the area had collapsed on the ground at the same time. "Ugh … it's the Turks. They're protesting by beating their cooking pots on their balconies. It's the last thing we need after escaping a war," Baklawa grumbled. As he knocked on the door he called out, "Mama Nabila, open up, I've got Furat with me, the one I told you about."

I will call Mama Nabila "she" as she asked, but she was born as a boy into a Christian family in Karrada in Baghdad. She fled to Istanbul with her brother when she was in her early thirties after the war in Iraq in 2003. They were supposed to escape to Sweden together, but while they were on the Turkish shore waiting for a boat, her brother spotted her in a nearby cave sucking off one of the smugglers. Mama Nabila assured her brother she had been forced into it, but her brother didn't buy it. He attacked her and swore in front of everyone present that he would kill her. Mama Nabila fled to Istanbul with that same smuggler and remained in hiding, terrified, until she was certain her brother had left Turkey. Once she was safe, she settled down in Istanbul and began sleeping with the smuggler gangs. They enjoyed fondling her soft, white, compact body, kissing and nibbling her full chest, and fucking her prominent behind, all the while ignoring her male member; in return they would pay her enough for a shawarma and a beer. In time it became her profession. She began to make the rounds of Istanbul's parks after midnight to pick up clients, especially in Fatih and Aksaray, all men who had no chance of finding sex except with a sex worker. As she became settled in this career she rented a small house in the backstreets of Cihangir and called it Selamlik.

Mama Nabila's Selamlik occupied a strategic position in the middle of Cihangir. It was right by the gay bars, the hammams, the sauna, and the lane of cross-dressers, where a sense of freedom led those in the know to nickname it "Istiklal" Street. Most of its patrons were drawn from smugglers, taxi drivers, elderly men, and tourists. As the wars in the Middle East spread, the Arab Spring bloomed in Mama Nabila's Selamlik. The escaping, the frightened, the concealed—all of them crowded into Turkey from Syria, Egypt, Bahrain, Yemen, Iraq, and Libya. Mama Nabila lay in wait for them wherever they could possibly go, from the Cihangir sauna to Hammam Fairuz Agha, where you could meet other men who loved men. Clients multiplied, the market was constantly in motion, and eventually Mama Nabila could no longer satisfy the desires of all her clients by herself; she had to fill the gap with someone she trusted. She searched among the newcomers to Istanbul, focusing on those under twenty, and eventually landed on Baklawa. She plucked him out of the lap of some old man in Cheero and gave him the name Baklawa because he was so sweet and his white flesh so tender and soft. She brought him into Selamlik in girls' clothes and announced him to the patrons as authentic Syrian cuisine. Mama Nabila's Selamlik was more than just beds to have sex on—it was also a secret office where human trafficking deals were struck. Within its rooms, the Waiting met with smugglers, and journeys were coordinated via Mama Nabila. Clients deposited their money with her and as soon as the boat moved off the Turkish shore (without any guarantee of the journey's success), the smugglers would collect the money from Mama Nabila—after she had taken her cut.

As we walked down the stairs, my blood pressure fell with every step. It was like descending into a grave. Despite the heat, my body trembled. "Welcome! Welcome to Selamlik," Mama Nabila boomed in an Iraqi accent and a feminine voice. She extended a plump arm adorned with bracelets and held her hand up to my lips. I kissed it and tasted dried cat food. "Women are forbidden from entering ... This selamlik is not a haremlik," she teased Baklawa, who was still wearing his dress. I couldn't work out how old Mama Nabila was but she seemed young. She had a round face with a sharp nose and puffy lips. Her head was large, and her hair was short and thick. She had left her soft, white face free of makeup, and she had thin eyebrows that looked as though they were drawn on with ballpoint pen. Her white flesh and full belly were enclosed in a red minidress, and her solid thighs appeared to be snow-white within the black fishnet tights. She wasn't wearing any shoes. Mama Nabila brought me into the selamlik, as hot and damp as a sauna, and waved me towards the brown leather sofa in the centre of the room. Then she vanished behind a short linen curtain printed with three Japanese women in kimonos who looked as though they were gossiping about us behind their fans.

"It's still too early … The smugglers won't be here before dawn, when they're totally drunk," Baklawa complained, struggling out of his high heels. He leaned on the wall and raised his right leg in the air, trying to rub the toes that were stuck together. "Baklawa!" thundered Mama Nabila from behind the Japanese ladies. Baklawa stepped over his high heels and looked back at me as he rubbed his fingers and thumb together. Evidently, Mama Nabila wanted to take his earnings from his earlier commission at a client's house.

As soon as I sat down on the brown leather sofa, a black cat came out from underneath it, yawned in my face, and followed Baklawa. The underground waiting room featured walls painted black and pink and a crumbling wooden floor. Near the top of the room there was a long, thin window painted over with black. High above my head, a weak yellow lightbulb dangled from a cable. Overhead, a ceiling fan turned like an ancient noria wheel. The sound of a powerful shower mingled with the voice of Mama Nabila as she chatted in Turkish and roared with laughter— she seemed to be talking on the phone.

I sat with my arms crossed and my back against the sofa, waiting, although I didn't know what for—the arrival of the smugglers who would come later? for Mama Nabila to finish her conversation? or for Baklawa to finish in the shower? It felt like waiting for the dentist—I would pay up and wait to feel pain, perhaps concentrated pain, for a short time, hoping that it would lessen the remaining pain long-term. The sound of ferocious beating against the outside door pulled me from my thoughts—I wondered if it was a raid. "Coming," Baklawa called from inside.

Baklawa hurried out from behind the Japanese women. He had taken off his wig and scrubbed off his makeup, and now he was wearing denim hotpants that showed off his smooth legs, and a sparkly T-shirt that made his torso look like a disco ball. As soon as Baklawa opened the door, a tall, skinny man stormed inside, his eyes flashing. I got up off the sofa and stood stock-still. The man grabbed Baklawa's neck with both hands and pushed him against the wall. "Mama Nabila," croaked Baklawa. With one hand, the man took the scruff of Baklawa's neck from behind and held it tight in his fist; with the other, he gave Baklawa a hard slap. The man then dragged Baklawa by his collar and secured his arm around Baklawa's neck. Now Baklawa couldn't speak or even breathe, but he began to punch the man in the stomach in the hope he would let him go. I put my hand over my mouth and watched the fight. Mama Nabila thrust the curtain aside, swept through the middle of the Japanese women, and tried to free Baklawa from the man's arms. The three of them turned into a thick knotted mass rolling all over the place.

Finally Baklawa was freed and he fell to the ground, trying to catch his breath and staring at me pop-eyed.

He stood and ran outside. The man shoved Mama Nabila into the wall, then drew a knife from behind his waist and raised it to my face, all the while screaming in Turkish. His face was wolfish. I leapt onto the sofa, and the ceiling fan nearly chopped my head off. "Get out, run away," yelled Mama Nabila in her real, much gruffer voice, pulling the man towards her.

I fled to safety.

The air outside was toxic from tear gas. Baklawa was standing at the top of the alleyway—I could see his outfit glittering in the darkness. Eyes burning, I hurried over to him. He told me he was only crying because of the tear gas. "But tear gas is no problem for anyone who's escaped bombings and bullets and mines and explosions and knives. Do you have a cigarette?" When I said no, he let out a sardonic laugh and said, "Do you want to be a clean meal for the fish when you drown in the Mediterranean?" I told him to get further away from the house before that crazy man came out, but he interrupted me: "You mean Sinan? No, no, don't worry. Mama Nabila will give him some money to calm him down and then she'll convince him to follow her to bed." Then he added, "Believe me, Sinan's nothing to worry about … The scary one is Mama Nabila. Didn't you know that? Maybe it's time for me to travel to Europe, maybe on the same boat as you." Despite the tension and the security agents who had encircled Taksim Square and spread out across Cihangir that night in response to the protests against the Turkish regime, Baklawa was determined to stay with me and tell me the story of the madman Sinan. He suggested going dancing in Cheero and returning to Selamlik together later.

Sinan the taxi driver was infatuated with Baklawa's deliciousness. He had met Baklawa in one of the red rooms. At first he was just a client like any other, paying for a tender embrace and a few gentle words. But what Baklawa didn't realise was that Sinan was suffering from an acute lack of warmth and kindness—and moreover, he was unstable. Sinan fell madly in love with Baklawa and began refusing to let him sleep with other clients, hunting him through the streets and party spots. Sinan paid Baklawa everything he earned from driving his taxi, on the condition that Baklawa didn't sleep with other men. Baklawa mentioned a staggering sum—I simply couldn't believe it. Once Sinan had emptied his pockets, he no longer had enough money to control Baklawa, so he resorted to violence instead. Any movement of Baklawa's was considered a betrayal. The struggle between the two men escalated until there were multiple death threats, although Baklawa didn't take these threats seriously because he believed Sinan was good at heart. What he hadn't expected was that Mama Nabila would fall in love with Sinan. Mama Nabila wished she were in Baklawa's place, and dreamed of taking Sinan and all the money she could gather and vanishing. Sinan couldn't bear Mama Nabila, however; she was the one who paid him to sleep with her, and she increased the sum every time in the hope that he would return her love.

Baklawa told me every detail of this story in a cool manner on our way to Cheero, as if it were gossip about some strangers and had nothing to do with him. At the entrance to Cheero he took an old-looking stick of gum out of his pocket. He broke it in two pieces, gave me one, and flicked the other in his mouth.

In Cheero everything was red, sticky, and hot—faces, heads, necks, my hands, backs, chests, and shoulders. Even the curtains, the glasses, the drinks, and the walls were red. It was like being in a slaughter pit. In Istanbul they call dark rooms "red rooms." When the disco ball in the ceiling stops turning and the faint red light comes on, it's an invitation from the owners to their patrons to consume each other's flesh. I didn't understand what Baklawa said to me because of the loud beat and the ringing echo of clinking glasses and men's tongues dancing together in different languages, until he yelled in my ear, "Ten minutes and we'll go back to Selamlik, the smugglers will be coming!" His breath smelled of strawberry. I wanted to buy him a drink but he refused. Instead he turned around and found an empty beer glass on a table. He picked it up and turned his goggling eyes towards an old man and chewed his gum to the rhythm of the beat. He plucked at the flimsy collar of his T-shirt to show more of his back and shoulders, and began to shuffle his feet forwards like a belly dancer, swaying his skinny hips towards the man, his empty beer glass in his fingertips—Baklawa's signal to prospective clients that he was open for business. The collar of his cheap T-shirt revealed the angel wings tattooed on his back.

Suddenly all the lights in the room went out apart from the dark red glow. "Where did Baklawa go? I saw him with you just now." Mama Nabila appeared in front of me without warning, her white flesh imprisoned in the arms of a huge man whose eyes I didn't dare meet. I could see the man's wrinkled hands cupped like a bra, covering Mama Nabila's nipples. Wordlessly I pointed in the direction of the heap of sparkles on the ground. Baklawa was squatting on his knees, his head hidden between a man's thighs. He took his head out of the man's trousers and took a deep breath.

That was the last time I saw Baklawa's face. At the end of the night they found his body, stabbed right between the wings in the middle of his back and flung into a corner of the red room. Mama Nabila vanished after this incident.

I didn't witness the crime. I had decided to go back to where I was staying when I saw that Baklawa was drunk and there was no hope of getting back to Selamlik that night. I was staying in a men-only hostel in Aksaray while I waited in Istanbul. It was a selamlik, but of a different kind. A selamlik that was wretched and boring compared to Mama Nabila's. Fathers, men, and boys populated it, all looking forward to meeting the Prophet Moses so he could part the seas and help them cross safely to the other side. Turkey was like the barzakh for Syrians, somewhere between the first life and immortality. We were waiting to move on, and we didn't know what was waiting for us on the other shore, heaven or hell.

LERI PRICE is an award-winning literary translator of contemporary Arabic fiction. Price's translation of Khaled Khalifa's *Death Is Hard Work* was a finalist for the 2019 National Book Award for Translated Literature and winner of the 2020 Saif Ghobash Banipal Prize for Arabic Literary Translation. Her translation of *Planet of Clay* by influential Syrian writer Samar Yazbek, also published by World Editions, was a finalist for the 2021 National Book Award for Translated Literature. Price's other recent translations include *Sarab* by award-winning writer Raja Alem and *Where the Wind Calls Home* by Samar Yazbek.

Book Club Discussion Guides on our website.

World Editions promotes voices from around the globe by publishing books from many different countries and languages in English translation. Through our work, we aim to enhance dialogue between cultures, foster new connections, and open doors which may otherwise have remained closed.

Also available from World Editions:

On the Isle of Antioch
Amin Maalouf
Translated by Natasha Lehrer
"A beguiling, lyrical work of speculative fiction by
a writer of international importance."
—*Kirkus Reviews*, *Starred Review*

About People
Juli Zeh
Translated by Alta L. Price
A novel about the social and very private conse-
quences of the pandemic, written by Germany's #1
bestselling author Juli Zeh.

Fowl Eulogies
Lucie Rico
Translated by Daria Chernysheva
"Disturbing, compelling, and heartbreaking."
—CYNAN JONES, author of *The Dig*

My Mother Says
Stine Pilgaard
Translated by Hunter Simpson
"A hilarious queer break-up story."
—OLGA RAVN, author of *The Employees*

We Are Light
Gerda Blees
Translated by Michele Hutchison
"Beautiful, soulful, rich, and relevant."
—*Libris Literature Prize*

On the Design

As book design is an integral part of the reading experience, we would like to acknowledge the work of those who shaped the form in which the story is housed.

Tessa van der Waals (Netherlands) is responsible for the cover design, cover typography, and art direction of all World Editions books. She works in the internationally renowned tradition of Dutch Design. Her bright and powerful visual aesthetic maintains a harmony between image and typography, and captures the unique atmosphere of each book. She works closely with internationally celebrated photographers, artists, and letter designers. Her work has frequently been awarded prizes for Best Dutch Book Design.

The cover photo was shot by Maja Kristin Nylander, a visual artist and photographer based in Göteborg, Sweden. Nylander works with series of images based on personal experiences of presence and absence. Caring and carrying are central themes in Nylander's work.

The font used for *Selamlik* written in the Roman alphabet on the cover is called Tungsten. It was designed by Tobias Frere-Jones and Jonathan Hoefler. The Tungsten typeface is a family of compact, modular sans serifs, a style colorfully known to sign painters as "gaspipe lettering." The font first appeared on the Bravo television network in 2004.

Cover designer Tessa van der Waals intertwined Tungsten with a contemporary Arabic font called Greta Arabic. The original Greta Pro (Latin) was conceived by Peter Bil'ak in 2012, and the Arabic version was designed by Kristyan Sarkis and published in 2015. Both fonts spell *Selamlik*, expressing unity but also the inner conflict of the main character, in whom the Western and Eastern worlds collide, unite, and clash. For Tessa van der Waals, the belly button is the center of the photo, and she likes the playful way in which it is framed by the two typefaces.

Euan Monaghan (United Kingdom) is responsible for the typography and careful interior book design.

The text on the inside covers and the press quotes are set in Circular, designed by Laurenz Brunner (Switzerland) and published by Swiss type foundry Lineto.

All World Editions books are set in the typeface Dolly, specifically designed for book typography. Dolly creates a warm page image perfect for an enjoyable reading experience. This typeface is designed by Underware, a European collective formed by Bas Jacobs (Netherlands), Akiem Helmling (Germany), and Sami Kortemäki (Finland). Underware are also the creators of the World Editions logo, which meets the design requirement that "a strong shape can always be drawn with a toe in the sand."

Printed in the USA
CPSIA information can be obtained
at www.ICGtesting.com
JSHW022049290224
58353JS00002B/11